"The light shines in the darkness, and the darkness has not overcome it."

-John 1:5 (NIV)

MYSTERIES *of* LANCASTER COUNTY

Another's Treasure

Garage Sale Secret

An Unbroken Circle

Mixed Signals

Stamp of Approval

Plain Beauty

The Ties That Bind

Seek & Ye Shall Find

Lights! Camera! Christmas!

A Slowly Developing Story

Pride and Pettiness

By Any Other Name

Beg, Borrow, or Steal

Lilacs, Lavender, and Lies

Summer Harvest Secrets

Collateral Damage

Arson, Plain and Simple

ARSON, PLAIN AND SIMPLE

MYSTERIES *of* LANCASTER COUNTY

Kathleen Y'Barbo

Guideposts

Danbury, Connecticut

ARSON, PLAIN AND SIMPLE

DEDICATION

For the Artists and the Dreamers!

CHAPTER ONE

Here we go again. Mary knew that suffering for her art sometimes meant sitting on a lawn chair on a hot August day while shoppers milled about and haggled over the prices of her hand-painted postcards and oil paintings. But she didn't have to like it. Here she was, a first-time exhibitor at Lancaster's First Saturday Art Festival, a monthly celebration of artists and their work, hoping she could earn enough to make the day worthwhile without spending her profits on all the other unique pieces being sold all around her.

She'd just completed a purchase of a lovely hand-painted vest covered in roses and summer flowers from the sweet lady in the booth next to her when she spied a familiar face. At least she thought the tall silver-haired fellow with the athletic build and lopsided smile looked familiar.

When he stopped in front of her booth and aimed those deep brown eyes in her direction, Mary knew for certain that her high school friend had returned.

"I like that painting of the Classen barn," he said. "But could I order one just like it in a bigger size? I've got an empty space on my mantel, and it would be perfect there."

"Jake Miller," she exclaimed as she jumped out of her lawn chair so fast that she sent it tumbling backward. "The last time

I saw your face, you were on my television screen dressed in a baseball uniform and pitching in the World Series."

She and Jakob, as he was known back then, had been good friends since childhood. When Jakob was in his last year of *rumspringa*, he wasn't sure whether he wanted to return to his Amish faith or not. He'd always loved playing baseball as a child, but until a scout spied him throwing a ball against the Classens' barn hard enough to break a board, he had no thought of continuing to play after the end of his rumspringa.

Jakob listened to what the scout had to say and ended up in the major leagues as a pitcher. Now known as Jake Miller, he had long ago retired after a successful career. Whatever had happened in his personal life since the last time she saw him on her television screen had definitely agreed with him.

He gave her a sheepish grin and then let his gaze study the length of her. "That was quite a few years ago. You, however, look exactly the same, Mary Classen. How is that possible?"

"Mary Baxter now. And Jake, I was sorry to hear about Ellen's struggle with cancer." She put her hand on his arm. "How long has she been gone?"

"I appreciate that," he said. "It's been four years, but I still miss her. I'm just here to see Caleb."

Caleb Miller was the little brother Jakob used to take with him almost everywhere he went. Caleb's birth had been hard on his mother, and she never fully recuperated. Thus, once the little boy was big enough to follow Jakob around, that's what he did. Despite the ten-year age gap, Jakob not only tolerated the little guy's antics, but he loved him dearly.

According to Caleb, when he reached his rumspringa years, Jake invited him to come and stay with him in New York City. By then Jake had left baseball for medical school, a fact that had been emblazoned on the front page of not only the *New York Times*, but it had also made the local papers. But as Caleb told her the last time he delivered items for sale at Secondhand Blessings, Bird-in-Hand was where he was born, and Bird-in-Hand was where he would stay.

Last month he'd married an Amish woman named Anna whose family lived near Pittsburgh. Anna and her oldest sister, Abigail, were close, and the new bride insisted her sister join her in Bird-in-Hand and live in the *dawdy haus* at Anna's new home with Caleb.

Mary had learned all of this from Rachel Fischer, the Amish woman she and her sisters counted as a close friend as well as a part-time employee of Secondhand Blessings. She'd also learned that either Jake had not been invited to the wedding, or he'd chosen not to come.

Either way, Mary was stunned to see him here now.

"I didn't accidentally stroll by and find you, Mary. Elizabeth told me where you'd be. Do you have time to have coffee later? Or dinner depending on how late you'll be here? I'd like to talk to you about Caleb."

"Why me?" she asked. "After you left, I didn't stay in touch with him or your parents. I rarely see Caleb other than when he comes to deliver items for sale at the store, so I don't know what sort of help I would be."

"You're the sort of help I need." He paused. "Did you go to Caleb's wedding?"

She shook her head. "No. I understand it was a strictly Amish affair."

"Ah," he said, bitterness intoning his voice. "That answers my question." He shook his head.

Mary thought she knew where this was coming from. "So you weren't invited?" she asked gently.

He shrugged. "Caleb sent me an email. Apparently he's got a phone at the furniture shop now. And a computer."

"Yes," Mary said. "Many elders of Amish churches have allowed phones and computers in the workplace as long as they aren't brought into their homes." She paused. "So you were invited, but you didn't attend."

"No," he said softly. "Caleb hinted that his bride and her family might be uncomfortable having me there. I didn't have to be a genius to read between the lines and get the message."

"I'm sorry," she told him. "Is it possible Caleb was just being protective of her?"

He let out a long breath. "Even if he was, why would he marry a woman who feels she needs to be protected from his brother?"

"I've met Anna, and she is very old-school Amish. Whether it was Caleb's brother or not, my guess is she would be reluctant to have someone there who chose to leave the church."

"I didn't leave the church," he snapped. He shook his head. "I'm sorry. Look, I left the church before I was baptized, so I didn't technically leave, and I wasn't shunned by our community. Apparently that little detail doesn't matter to my sister-in-law."

"And that's driven a wedge into your relationship with Caleb?"

"Not yet, but if Anna has her way, I'm sure it will." He paused. "That's why I came to you, Mary. I need some help. You know how much I love my brother."

She smiled. "I remember him tagging along wherever you went. He was your shadow, and I'm not sure which of you liked that more."

Jake chuckled. "Probably me, but then Caleb would say it was him."

"Then a wife won't come between you," she said.

"She already has."

"Yes, I suppose you're right." Mary paused. "But I'm confused as to how I can help you."

"I figure if you're anything like you were back then, you're pretty well liked around here, and maybe you can speak to those who can encourage Anna to speak to me."

"I don't know about that," she said. "But I do have a number of Amish friends. And I always did like Caleb."

"He speaks fondly of you too. He said he's been providing a few pieces from his shop to sell at your store."

"He has, and we're grateful. His pieces always sell quickly."

"So can I ask you a huge favor?"

Mary grinned. "That depends on what the favor is."

"Would you come with me to pay a visit to the newlyweds?" He rubbed his chin. "I figure if you're with me Anna will be more polite than she might be to family."

Mary didn't have to think about it twice. "If you believe it will help, then sure. I would love to." She considered her other responsibilities. "I won't be here past two, but it's going to take at least an hour to repair what the heat has wilted."

"How about I pick you up at your house at three thirty? That way we can pay a visit and then I'll take you to dinner after. I have a place all picked out."

Dinner with Jake Miller? Now that was a whole other thing.

She hesitated. "Just to talk about whatever it is we encounter at Caleb's house."

"And to make sure the restaurant isn't awful." He winked at her.

"Awful?" Mary frowned at him. "Where are you taking me, Jake Miller?"

"It's not awful," he assured her. "I've read the reviews. I've just never been there before."

Mary laughed. "Well, all right then."

Jake grinned. "The restaurant seating is outside, so dress casually."

"Now you have me curious. That's all you're going to say? You want to see if it's any good, and be prepared to eat outdoors?"

He nodded. "Yes, that's all."

She chuckled. "I have just one suggestion: don't use that line on anyone but me, or you'll never get a date."

His grin was dazzling. "Just like old times, Mary. I'm sorry we lost touch."

"Me too."

A man in a plain blue ball cap, dark T-shirt, and jeans had been hovering nearby during the entire conversation. He caught Mary's attention and smiled.

"Looks like you've got a fan," Jake said. "I'll make myself scarce."

"More likely *you* do," she said.

"No, a dude knows when another dude is checking a woman out." He took a moment. "And he's checking you out. Or your artwork. And speaking of artwork, I was serious about commissioning a painting of the Classen barn. We can talk about it tonight." He glanced over at the man in the blue cap. "Yes, definitely checking you out. See you later, gator."

"After a while, crocodile," she said without thinking. They both laughed.

He leaned over and hugged her, and for a moment, Mary was seventeen again. Then he stepped back and offered her that lopsided grin. Without a word, he loped off into the crowd and disappeared.

"Hello," she said when the man approached. "How can I help you?"

He nodded in the direction where her dinner date had gone. "Was that Jake Miller? I used to try to pitch like him when he played for the Yankees and I was a skinny teenager in Brooklyn."

"It was," she said. "If you hurry you can probably catch him."

He shook his head. "That's tempting, but no, I'm actually here to see you, Mrs. Baxter." He studied her. "You are Mary Classen Baxter, aren't you?"

"I am. How can I help you?"

"Augie Meyers," he said as he stuck out his hand and offered her a business card. "I own the Bird-in-Hand Gallery in Philly."

"Bird-in-Hand? Interesting name for a Philadelphia art gallery." She grinned as she looked down at the card. Instead of the familiar Amish logo that represented her hometown, the image of a man's hand clutching an escaping rooster was emblazoned on the corner of the card. "And you have an interesting card too, Mr. Meyers."

"Augie, please." He shrugged. "Mr. Meyers is my father. It's not my art, but I have permission from the owner to use it."

Mary tucked the card into her pocket. "I'm sure there's a story behind it. And please, call me Mary."

He waved away the statement about his logo. "There is, actually, but I doubt you want to hear an old man's story about a chicken dinner."

"Now you absolutely must tell me," she insisted. "Not that I believe for a minute that you're an old man."

"Oh, not me. My grandfather," he said with a twinkle in his eye. "Although I have a twelve-year-old daughter who would definitely call me old." Augie paused. "The short version is my grandparents met over a sixty-cent chicken dinner at Bird-in-Hand restaurant on Seventh Avenue in Philadelphia. My grandfather was just a kid, but they hired him to deliver since he had a working bicycle and very little idea of what a delivery boy ought to be paid. His first job was to take an order of boxed chicken dinners out for delivery. Since this is a love story, you've probably guessed that the pretty girl who answered the door was my grandmother."

"That's so sweet," Mary exclaimed.

"Grandpa's employers didn't think so. When he finally returned to the restaurant three hours later, they sacked him on the spot. He swiped a menu on his way out as a memento of the day he met his future wife. That menu was my first piece of framed art. And the money I inherited from my grandfather funded the gallery I own now. So, in homage to him, I named it after the Bird-in-Hand Restaurant. It took a while, but I tracked down the rights to the logo, and here I am."

Mary smiled. "Yes. Here you are. So what brings you here? Have you come to check out the other Bird-in-Hand?"

The gallery owner matched her grin. "Actually, that's how you got on my radar, Mary. I follow what's being put out on the internet about my gallery. Last week, I got a Google alert that turned out not to be about my Bird-in-Hand art gallery but about this Bird-in-Hand arts festival. I followed the contributors' link until I found the photographs of your work." He paused. "I was impressed."

"Thank you."

He nodded to the table where her merchandise was displayed. "I'm buying pieces for my private collection, but I may put a few of these in the gallery to test my clients' interest. I think you have a rare talent."

CHAPTER TWO

Martha Classen Watts looked out the window of the small office just off the kitchen and watched as a hawk slowly circled over the nearby field. At her feet was Pal, their ornery but loveable border collie. While Pal snored, their dachshund, Tinkerbelle, lifted her head at the slightest sound to sniff the air or let out a yip. Butterscotch, their orange tabby cat, eyed the dogs warily from his perch above the filing cabinet and then yawned and went back to sleep.

She returned to her computer and the bread recipe she'd found. A few clicks later, and the printer jolted to life as she prepared to take the recipe to the kitchen. She would try it out for possible inclusion in the baked goods she made for the store next week.

At the sound of the printer, Tink lifted her head to bark at the unexpected noise. "Hush," she told the excitable dog. "It's just a recipe printing. If you're good I might just give you a treat when it's finished."

At the word *treat*, Pal sprang to life as if risen from the dead. He shook off sleep and then rested his chin on her leg, looking up at her with his best please-feed-me expression. Tink edged in as close as she could, lifting her little paws to rest them beside Pal's chin on Martha's leg. Meanwhile

Butterscotch stretched, surveyed the pair of begging canines, and then rolled over to go back to sleep.

Martha scratched the old dog behind the ears and patted Tink then stood. "All right, you two. I'll get you all a treat. But I only have a few minutes before I have to get back to the shop."

The pups scattered, heading for the door in anticipation of whatever treat awaited them. Martha stepped out into the hallway and nearly ran into Elizabeth.

"Oh!" she said as she collected herself. "I was just on my way back to the shop. I didn't hear you come in."

The dogs skittered into the hall from the kitchen to surround the oldest Classen sister. "It appears these two didn't either," Elizabeth said as she leaned down to give attention to each of them. "Rachel and Phoebe came in and are covering the store for a few minutes while I get a sandwich." She straightened up. "You'll never believe who came into the shop this morning."

Their store, Secondhand Blessings, sat on a part of the Classen property that bordered the road. The old barn had been turned into a shop by their grandparents years ago but had closed once the sisters' parents' health ceased to allow them to operate it. The sisters had reopened Secondhand Blessings more than a year ago, and it had become a thriving enterprise that kept all three of them busy.

Martha nodded toward the kitchen. "Follow me. I'm going to check and see if I have the ingredients for a new recipe. You can tell me all about it while you make your sandwich." Tink looked back at her and barked. "Oh, and give these two a treat. Apparently Tink thinks I've forgotten."

"No problem." Elizabeth reached for the tin of dog treats, capturing Tink's attention instantly. Pal merely sat and waited. He knew he'd be rewarded for his patience. Tink, however, had no idea what patience was.

They shared a laugh at Tink's antics as Martha dropped the recipe on the counter and moved toward the sink. "So, who came into the shop?"

Elizabeth looked over at her with a broad grin. "Jakob Miller. Remember him? And guess what he wanted?"

"Of course I remember him. I assume he wasn't looking for one of those new quilted tea cozies that Rachel brought in yesterday," Martha joked.

"He wanted to speak with Mary," Elizabeth said, eyes wide. "And let me just tell you that the skinny teenager turned out to be quite a handsome man."

Martha shook her head as she turned on the water and reached for the soap. "That's not news. His face was plastered to the television screen for years when he played baseball."

Elizabeth waved away the comment. "I know, but he's even more handsome these days. He's a doctor now. An orthopedic surgeon, no less. He lives in New York, and here's the best part. He's a widower."

"Elizabeth," Martha said sharply. "How is that the best part? He lost his wife. Have some compassion."

"I didn't mean it that way," she said. "It's just that he's here in Bird-in-Hand, he's asking for Mary, and he's single."

Martha dried her hands and then folded the towel and replaced it on the counter. "Oh," she said as she considered

Elizabeth's statement. "Yes, that is newsworthy. Did he say why he was looking for Mary?"

"Yes. He said he wanted her to go with him to see Caleb. That has to mean something, doesn't it? I know they were just friends way back when, but I always thought if she hadn't gotten married right out of high school she and Jakob might have eventually gotten together."

"They were just friends," Martha said. "And reading anything else into this visit is just not wise. Obviously he's here to see Caleb."

"Well, good luck with that," said Elizabeth. "I doubt he'll be able to get past Anna."

"Yeah, she seems to be a bit on the prickly side," said Martha. "Maybe Jakob wants Mary for reinforcement. If anyone can win Anna over, it's our Mary."

Elizabeth snorted. "Maybe. If she wears a prayer *kapp* and apron. Otherwise, I'm afraid our little sister won't get much farther than the front porch."

Mary arranged the postcards on her table and tried to imagine her work in a gallery in Philadelphia. As a housewife in Indiana raising babies and puttering around with paint and canvas during their nap times, she'd never expected that her efforts would result in this. Dreamed, perhaps, but never expected.

Before she could collect herself, the gallery owner had gone to work sorting through her stacks of oil paintings. He'd already perused the ones hanging on display. She left him alone but watched with eager interest. During the next half hour Augie purchased half her stock and left her a business card and a promise to call soon with an order for some of her bigger pieces.

And though that was exciting, her mind kept returning to Jake Miller. Not the Jake Miller who stood before her at the arts festival but Jakob Miller, the teenager whose dreams took him far from Bird-in-Hand.

Two elderly ladies approached to admire a landscape painting, and she tucked her thoughts away to concentrate on the women and their questions about her wares. When the gates were finally closed and the last of the shoppers had gone, Mary had very little to take home.

She lifted her eyes to the heavens to give thanks for the blessing of a profitable day and then returned to her task of packing up what remained in her booth. The second of two boxes had been filled with painted goods when Bill Richmond hurried toward her.

Mary had known Bill easily as long as she'd known Jake. While Jake had gone out into the world and made a name for himself with his fastball, Bill had remained here in Lancaster and quietly made the world better through his kindness.

Bill glanced around to see the booth had been emptied then turned his attention to Mary. "I see I'm too late to help," he said, disappointment lacing his voice.

"Well, hello there," she said to her old friend. "You are, but that's because I only have these two boxes of things to take home."

"How about that?" he said. "You just about sold out. Not that I ought to be surprised. You're a talented woman, Mary."

"Thanks, Bill. You're pretty talented yourself. I'd like to talk to you about making some more frames for me. The ones you fixed up for this event are heading to Philadelphia right now."

His eyes widened. "All of them?"

"Every single one. But I've been here since the crack of dawn, and I'd like nothing better than to go home and take a hot shower. This Cinderella is about to turn into a pumpkin."

Bill reached for the first box, set it on the wheeled luggage rack, and then situated the second box on top of it. "Where's your carriage, milady?"

"I can get that," Mary protested.

"But then you'd miss out on spending time with me all the way from the tent to the car."

She did enjoy spending time with Bill. He was smart, helpful, and he never failed to make her smile.

"Follow me," she said with a chuckle.

They fell into conversation, and soon they reached the spot where she'd parked the car. After locating her keys, Mary stepped back while Bill loaded the boxes and the wheeled luggage rack then closed the trunk.

Straightening, he met her gaze and offered a smile and an exaggerated bow. "Your carriage is ready for you, Cinderella."

"Thank you very much, Prince Charming." Mary curtsied, and they both laughed. "No matter how tired I am, it always seems like you make me feel better. Thanks, Bill."

His expression sobered. "I'm glad I can do that for you."

Bill shifted positions. Mary got the impression he had more to say. After a moment, when he remained silent, she opened the car door. She climbed inside and snapped her seat belt.

"Thanks again," she told him.

"Say, Mary, do you have plans for this evening?"

She shrugged. "I'm headed out to visit Caleb Miller. Jake is in town, and he asked if I would go with him to meet Anna."

"That's an interesting idea," Bill said. "If she has trouble meeting one *Englischer*, I don't know how two would be any better. But I didn't realize he was back in Bird-in-Hand."

"Just to visit, I believe." She paused. "I'm sorry, but I need to hurry home and clean up. I doubt Anna and Caleb would want to welcome a visitor who's been sitting out in the heat all day."

Bill grinned. "You look just fine, Mary, but then you always do. I'll call you in a day or two to talk about the frames. I've got some ideas for using different woods, but I want to run them by you before I finalize them."

"That sounds fine."

"Or I could stop by the store," he offered as she turned her key in the ignition.

"That would be great," she told him over the sound of the car's engine. "You know how forgetful I can be."

"I'll see you tomorrow," he said just before she closed the door.

As Mary drove away, she glanced in the rearview mirror to catch Bill watching her. It always struck her at times like these how much he looked like a scruffier version of Harrison Ford. Rakish grin and just the right twinkle in his eyes to make her smile.

That was her Bill. *Her Bill?* Mary pushed away the thought. He lifted his hand to wave, and she did the same. Though she was exhausted, her smile lingered long after the image of Bill was gone. She'd be glad to see him in church tomorrow.

Mary returned to the farmhouse she shared with her sisters and hurried inside to drop her purse on the table by the door. Elizabeth and Martha met her at the door. At least Elizabeth had thought of bringing a lemonade to the inquisition that began the minute her foot crossed the threshold.

"I assume Jakob Miller found you." Elizabeth handed her the lemonade. "He certainly hasn't changed much." She smiled. "Other than to fill out and allow his hair to turn gray, neither of which I have a problem with. In fact, he wears his age well."

Mary took a sip and then shook her head. "Don't get any ideas. He's worried about Caleb and says he needs my help meeting Anna." She put the cold glass to her forehead, relishing the icy water that had condensed on the side. "He thinks Anna didn't want him at the wedding."

"He's right about that," Martha said. "But I wonder what he thinks you can do?"

"All I know is that he said he needed my help overcoming whatever issues he believes his new sister-in-law has with him. He'll be here in a little over an hour."

Elizabeth smirked at her. "So is this a date?"

"It's not a date." Mary finished her lemonade and then pressed past her sisters to walk into the kitchen and deposit the glass in the sink. "As I said, he needs my help with Anna. He believes she's influencing Caleb against him because he's no longer Amish. Jake just wants to see if I can help smooth things out. That's all I know."

"Oh, stop teasing her, Lizzie," Martha said. "I think Jake is smart in enlisting Mary's help. I don't see anything except a friend calling on a friend to help smooth things out."

"Exactly." Mary nodded toward the stairs. "I'm going upstairs to get cleaned up. If Jake gets here before I come down, please don't say anything embarrassing. Tonight I'm doing a favor for a friend, and that's all."

"I was just teasing," Elizabeth said. "I didn't mean to make you mad."

"I'm not mad. Just sensitive about the subject, I guess." She paused. "And truly, I don't want to be embarrassed. He came to me to ask me to help him. I don't want him to think I'm taking advantage of that."

"In all seriousness," Martha said, "if I were to think of anyone as a potential boyfriend for you, it would not be Jake Miller."

"Well, that's good to hear." Mary was halfway up the stairs when a thought occurred. She turned around to face her sisters again. "Who would it be?"

"Bill," both sisters said in unison. Then they looked at each other and giggled.

Mary shook her head. Bill was just a friend too. She thought of how he made her smile every single time she saw him. He was a friend, wasn't he?

"What a question. Of course he is," Mary muttered as she headed for the shower.

CHAPTER THREE

Elizabeth watched Mary disappear up the stairs then picked up her phone and tucked it into her pocket. Martha was already in the kitchen, so she called out to her.

"I'm going to head back to the shop to help Rachel and Phoebe."

Pans rattled in the kitchen and then silence. "All right," Martha said, "I'll be right behind you."

"Sounds good," she called as she shut the door behind her and made her way to the shop. She greeted Rachel and Phoebe and thanked them for their help before sending them home. The shop would be closing up soon anyway. Not too long after they left, Martha walked in and headed to the children's section to tidy up.

Elizabeth had just finished dusting some kitchenware when her phone rang. She saw the name of the caller and smiled.

"Hello there," she said to John. "I didn't expect to hear from you until after your shift ended today."

"I'm calling on official business," he said. "I know the shop isn't closed just yet, but would you be able to leave a little early and meet me in town for coffee? I've got some questions about a case."

"How about I meet you at Un-Common Grounds?"

"I'm on my way," he said.

"All right," she said, "I'll race you."

He chuckled. "That'll be just fine. First one pays the bill."

After making sure Martha was okay with closing the shop on her own, she headed out to the coffee shop. As it turned out, they arrived in front of the little stone cottage turned coffee shop at almost the same time. Elizabeth pulled her car up next to John's squad car and smiled as she saw him look across at her and grin.

A few minutes later, with coffees ordered, they were seated at a table in the back of the room. John reached across the table to press his palm over her hand. "Thank you for seeing me on short notice."

She did her best to keep her eyes focused on the handsome policeman, but her mind was on the warmth of his hand atop hers. "You said you needed my help."

He leaned back, removing his hand from hers. "I do. I just left Masts' Furniture Store. There was an anonymous call regarding an argument between two Amish fellows, Caleb Miller and Amos Mast."

"Okay." Elizabeth shrugged. "I don't see what this has to do with me, but how can I help?"

"You know both Amos and Caleb, don't you?"

"Well, yes. Caleb is one of our suppliers at Secondhand Blessings. And everyone in Bird-in-Hand knows Amos. His parents own the furniture store, and we've all watched him grow up there. I guess if we're talking about the two of them as children, I also watched Caleb grow up, since he tagged along with his brother to our farm every chance he got."

"I heard Jakob was back in town." He paused. "Or I guess we call him Jake now."

"Yes, he came by the shop this morning to ask about Mary's whereabouts." She almost told him that Jake was now very likely on his way to pick Mary up for a visit and dinner, but she decided against it. "So again, what does all of this have to do with me?"

"I trust your impressions of people, Elizabeth," he said. "And I don't have any personal experience with either of these men."

"All right." She paused. "People argue, John. Why call the police, especially anonymously? Was one of them hurt by the other?"

"Not yet," John said. "But threats were made."

The waitress arrived with their coffees. He waited until she was gone to continue.

"Specifically, our anonymous caller said the men were arguing whether Caleb stole a design for a table from Amos or Amos stole it from Caleb."

Elizabeth took a sip of coffee. "That hardly sounds like the police should be involved."

"My boss had no intention of following up on it until the 911 call on a fire at Masts' Furniture went out this morning."

"Oh my goodness. I had no idea."

"The fire was limited to a dumpster filled with broken pieces of furniture and packing materials, but if it hadn't been seen and called in when it was, it could have easily jumped to the building." John paused to take a sip of coffee. "Add that to the fact that Wednesday there was an act of arson at an Amish-owned business in Lancaster, and that anonymous tip has a whole new level of importance."

"I heard about that fire at Yoder's Paint and Art Supply," Elizabeth said, "but I had no idea it was arson. I've gone with Mary there before. The owners are such nice people."

"You didn't know because the arson folks in Lancaster haven't released that information yet. There was another fire two weeks ago at a shop that sold hardware over in New Holland. Also arson and a similar scenario. Fire in the trash can set the rest of the building on fire."

Elizabeth glanced around and then returned her attention to John as she lowered her voice. "Do you think there's a connection to Caleb or Amos?"

"I asked both shop owners to run the two men's names through their customer database."

"Let me guess. They got hits for both of them."

"Yes."

"That makes sense, I suppose. Paint and furniture go together, as does hardware and furniture."

John nodded. "And that brings me back to my original question." He shifted positions, his expression serious. "With what you know about Caleb Miller, would he do something like this? While you're considering that, is Amos Mast the type who would set a dumpster on fire to frame a guy he was mad at? And would either of them have a reason to settle other grudges that way?"

Elizabeth gave the questions some thought. "Caleb Miller has been nothing but kind and polite in his interactions with me. I don't know how he'd react in an argument, but I can say that based on what I have seen personally, I'd be shocked to find out that Caleb was behind that fire or any of the others."

"So you're saying you don't think he would send a message to the man he's just argued with by setting a fire?"

"No, absolutely not. In fact, I'm surprised he got into an argument at all. I've never seen him cross with anyone." Elizabeth shrugged. "I'm not saying that couldn't happen. I'm sure it does. But in my experience, I don't see him as a man who would set a fire to make a point."

"All right," John said. "Let's talk about Amos Mast. A couple of his employees were willing to admit he's a hothead sometimes, though none of them were willing to go on record about it."

"I don't know, John. We're a secondhand store, and Mama and Daddy's furniture suits us just fine at home, so I haven't had any reason to patronize Masts' Furniture or have any other professional dealings with Amos or his family."

John took another sip of coffee and set his mug back on the table. "I'm going to write this report as unfounded for now. Two men argued, and then a fire was set on the property associated with one of them. Any evidence of how that fire was set will be collected by the arson guys. If there's suspicion that this needs to be investigated further, then that's what I'll do."

Elizabeth sighed. "Honestly, John, if that fire was set intentionally, my guess is it was kids playing around and not some vendetta between two Amish men. It's August, and school is out, so parents don't always know where they are and what they're doing. Kids don't think about the consequences of their actions."

"I'm inclined to agree with you." He grinned. "Are you sure you haven't had any police training? You've got a way of thinking that's pretty logical."

"None at all," she said with a laugh. "But thank you. I'll take that as a compliment."

The door to the coffee shop opened, and a pair of women stepped inside. One of them, Julie Bettencourt, looked over in their direction and waved.

"Do you know her?" John asked.

"Yes, I do. Julie's husband owned a business that sources wood from old barns. When her husband died last year, she continued on, and she's now running the operation. Successfully, as I understand."

John cast a glance at Julie, who was now ordering her coffee at the counter. "That's impressive."

"More than you know," she said. "Julie was a stay-at-home mom who was never involved in the business. I'm very proud of what she's accomplished."

Julie walked their way with a smile on her face. Elizabeth rose to give her a hug. After making the introductions, she watched as John greeted her friend.

"It's nice to meet you, John." Julie turned to Elizabeth. "And it's always wonderful to see you, Elizabeth. My friend is waiting, so…" She took two steps away then turned back around. "Just one more thing. Could I ask you a question, John?"

At his nod, Julie continued. "This is entirely hypothetical, of course."

"Of course," he said as his gaze drifted toward Elizabeth and then went back to Julie.

"If a person had information on something somebody may have done that was illegal, would that person be obligated to report the other person's crime to the police?"

"Not necessarily. Sometimes it depends on your position. For example, if you're a physician, you have an obligation to call the police if a person meeting certain criteria comes in with a gunshot wound. And of course there arc many professions that are required to report a suspected case of child or elder abuse. Is there something you'd like to report?"

Her expression changed from pleasant to something unreadable. "Oh, uh, no. I was just asking for a friend. I'll tell her what you said."

"Are you sure there's not something you'd like to tell me?" he asked as he retrieved a business card from his pocket and handed it to her.

She tucked the card into her purse. "I'm sure, but it was very nice meeting you. Good to see you again, Elizabeth. Now, if you'll excuse me."

Julie hurried over to where her friend was seated and said something. Then she raced for the door and left.

"I wonder what that was about," Elizabeth said as she watched the door shut behind Julie. She returned her attention to John.

"I don't know," he said. "But I wouldn't be surprised if I get a call from her eventually."

"Do you think it's about the fire?" Elizabeth asked.

"It could be anything," he said. "Now, let's get back to talking about where I'm going to take you for dinner and possibly a movie afterward."

She laughed. "I don't believe we were talking about that."

"No?" He gave her a surprised look. "Well then, let's talk about it."

The drive to Caleb's farm took less than ten minutes. Though Mary had never been there, she knew the area well.

Jake's family had lived on this property, and he often spoke of it when they were kids. Back then it would have been out of the question to bring an *Englisch* friend home, especially a female friend.

A simple sign written in white paint on a black board announced the place to also be the home of Miller Furniture Makers. Beneath the name were smaller letters that stated: CUSTOM ORDERS TAKEN, INQUIRE WITHIN.

Jake drove past the sign, through the gate, and down an unpaved drive that led to a white two-story home that was distinctively Amish in design. The drive continued past the house to a smaller building, also white, that must be where Caleb did his furniture making. Beyond that, the drive wound around to end up at a barn not much unlike the one on the Classen property. Mary thought she caught sight of the edge of a dawdy haus on the far side of the main house.

There were cows in the pasture and a small herd of goats penned up in the distance. Chickens scurried away, and a rooster crowed from the fence as they stepped out of the car.

Mary turned to admire the landscape, which included a garden of herbs near the side door and patches of red geraniums and bright orange and yellow marigolds planted against the wide front porch. She swiveled to take in the rest of the property. Then she caught sight of Jake and froze.

He was standing completely still with his back straight and his eyes focused on something behind her. Mary turned to see what he was looking at and found only the Miller home in his line of sight.

Then it dawned on her. Jake had never returned home after he left to play professional baseball.

Until now.

Mary imagined what it must be like for Jake to come back here after all these years. She stayed very still and quiet so as not to disturb her friend's thoughts.

"*Bruder?* Is that you?"

Mary turned to see Caleb Miller leaning against the doorframe of his workshop, wearing a long black apron over his clothes. The youngest Miller shook his head and stepped out into the afternoon sunshine with a wide grin on his face.

"It is you. You are home. Oh, bruder!"

Jake turned toward him as if in slow motion. At first Mary thought he might remain standing right where he was. Then he let out a whoop and met Caleb halfway to gather him in an embrace.

With the Miller brothers occupied greeting one another, Mary studied them openly. Though she saw Caleb often, it occurred to her that she had never seen the grown-up version of Caleb with Jake.

Caleb was every inch as tall as Jake, but the younger Miller was lean, and the elder brother had the broad shoulders and muscled arms of an athlete. Silver colored Jake's once-dark hair while Caleb barely showed a touch of age at his temples. But when they both turned to look in her direction, the family resemblance was striking.

"He has not been breaking boards on your family's barn again, has he?" Caleb called to her with a chuckle.

"Not that I know of, but he hasn't been here long," she said.

Jake shook his head. "Will I ever live that down?"

"No," Mary and Caleb said in unison.

Caleb paused to shake the sawdust off his apron then nodded to Jake. "You will need to do the same if you are coming inside."

After Jake made a show of clearing the flakes of wood off his shirt, most of it in his brother's direction, Caleb declared them ready to go inside. He led Mary and Jake toward the house, and the brothers continued a commentary of what had changed and what had stayed the same over the years until they reached the front walk.

There Caleb paused again to embrace his brother. "I have prayed for you to come home, bruder. Now my prayers have been answered."

"It's your home now." Jake patted Caleb's shoulder. "Yours and Anna's. May you fill it with children who are as beautiful as their mother and don't look a thing like you."

The men fell into laughter, and then Caleb sobered, his hand on the door. "I do hope so, Jakob, but I have waited far too late in life to have a houseful like our sisters do."

Mary thought of the two Miller sisters, each of whom had at least a half-dozen children. The sisters had married brothers and moved to Florida, where they lived happily most of the year and came to visit their Bird-in-Hand relatives when the weather was warm.

"I understand they weren't at the wedding either," Jake said. "Will either of them be visiting soon?"

An uncomfortable look crossed Caleb's face. "Eventually, I am sure. Anna just needs some time to settle in, and then we will welcome guests." He nodded to the door. "Come. Let us go inside. It is warm out here."

Jake glanced over at Mary with a look that told her he was displeased with Caleb's response. When he returned his attention to Caleb, the door was open, and his brother had already stepped inside.

He motioned for Mary to follow Caleb, and she did. Stepping inside the Miller home was like taking a trip back in time. But then, that was her impression of every other Amish home she'd been in.

Missing, however, was the shine of the polished wood floors and the scent of linseed oil mixed with whatever delicious food was cooking in the kitchen. For there was almost always something delicious being prepared in an Amish kitchen when she visited.

Though it was only the middle of the afternoon, the expansive room was filled with gloom and smelled musty at best. Had she not known Caleb was a married man, she would have thought him to be single by the look of his home.

Jake didn't bother to hide his displeasure. "Where is Anna?"

"Anna is not here at the moment." Caleb hurried over to light a lamp then turned abruptly at the sound of a car coming up the drive. "Not her again." He frowned then quickly put on a neutral expression and stalked toward the door. "Make yourself at home. I need to handle this."

Mary stepped over to the window and watched as Julie Bettencourt got out of her car and headed toward Caleb. "She looks angry."

Jake moved to a spot beside her. "So does Caleb." He jiggled the catch and raised the window just in time to hear Julie yell, "—could burn your business down with you inside, and you would deserve it."

CHAPTER FOUR

After John left, Elizabeth remained at the table enjoying her coffee. Moments like this were a rare treat, and she intended to savor every second before she had to go back home to finish her chores.

John had to go back to the East Lampeter Police Station to write his report, so it would be a while before he picked her up for dinner. Dinner. She smiled at the thought. Elizabeth had come to enjoy the time she spent with the handsome police officer.

Catherine Randall stepped out from the kitchen and spied Elizabeth. She waved and headed toward the table. "Are you here alone?"

"No, I was just having coffee with a friend."

"If you're not about to leave, can I join you?" she asked.

"Yes, of course." Elizabeth waited until Catherine was seated and then continued. "Is everything all right?"

"Yes, absolutely. I've been meaning to call the store, but since you're here, I'll just ask you directly." Catherine paused to let out a long breath. "Have you ladies considered a wider reach for the treats you sell at Secondhand Blessings?"

Elizabeth sat back in her chair. "Never," she said. "Martha can only bake so many things in a day, and we sell out what she provides almost every time."

"There's a simple solution to that," she said. "Hire help and use a commercial kitchen." Before Elizabeth could respond, Catherine continued. "Look, I can see I've surprised you. Let me tell you what has me thinking about this. I have a friend who is looking to sell exactly the kind of facility that Martha would need, and she's got employees that would go with the deal if the buyer so chooses. It needs work, but that's factored into the price. With a little bit of imagination, the enterprise could add catering or even a storefront to the mix. The sky's the limit."

"Well, that's all very interesting, but I doubt Martha would want to pursue something like this. She's just a hobby baker and certainly has never mentioned any interest in anything like that."

Catherine shrugged. "Maybe because she never thought it was possible to be anything more than a hobby baker."

"I suppose that could be true."

"I can only say that my love of coffee was once a hobby."

Elizabeth smiled. "I'm very glad you pursued your hobby then."

Catherine reached into her apron pocket and pulled out a pen and an order form. After turning the form over, she scribbled a name and number then handed the paper to Elizabeth.

"Tell Martha to give Eunice a call if she's interested." Another shrug. "And if she's not, then no harm done. And she's welcome to call me here at the shop if she's interested in talking to someone who went for it."

"I'll do that."

Elizabeth tucked the paper into her purse while the conversation turned to other things. When her phone buzzed with a text, she looked down to see it was John messaging her with the start time of the movie they'd agreed on seeing.

She also saw it was much later than she thought.

"I'm so sorry to do this," she told Catherine, "but I've got to go."

They said their goodbyes, and Elizabeth hurried home to get ready for her dinner with John. Of course, she was running late, which completely distracted her, as did the fact that her clean towels had fallen off the clothesline and now lay on the ground, covered in grass clippings.

"Oh no," she groaned. She tossed her purse back into her car and gathered the damp towels. By the time she'd shaken them out and hung them back up, it was almost time for John to pick her up.

She retrieved her purse from where she'd left it in her car and hurried inside. Dropping her keys and purse on the table, Elizabeth called to Martha to let her know she'd returned then ran upstairs.

Mary couldn't believe her ears. She'd never seen this side of Julie before. Mary exchanged a worried glance with Jake. "What on earth? Julie is making threats. Should one of us go out there?"

"And do what?" Jake asked. "Caleb is standing up for himself."

She frowned. "I've never heard Julie talk like that. What do you think has made her so upset?"

"Whatever it is, it looks as if Caleb is settling her down."

Another glance out the window showed Mary that Caleb and Julie were now conversing in what appeared to be a more congenial tone. At least Julie wasn't shouting about arson anymore.

"Truly, Jake, something has to be terribly wrong. I've known Julie for years, and she's a very nice woman."

"Even nice women get angry," he offered.

"I suppose."

With Caleb outside and still engaged in conversation with Julie, Mary felt free to roam around inside. Not far, of course, because Jake was glued to his spot at the window watching his brother, but she did wander into the kitchen.

If there was any place in a home where a woman's touch showed, it was in her kitchen. At least that was what Mary had experienced in her frequent visits to the homes of Amish friends.

There would be cookbooks with well-worn pages and perhaps favorite recipes torn from newspapers or written on scraps of paper tucked here and there inside. Favorite spices would be lined up neatly near the stove, and there were usually herbs growing in a patch of sunlight near a window.

But there was none of that. No herbs, no cookbooks, and no sign that a woman had graced this room in a very long time.

Mary sighed. "Oh, Caleb, what's going on?"

"I was wondering the same thing."

Mary jumped and whirled around to see Jake watching her carefully. "You nearly scared me to death," she said as she clutched her chest. "I didn't hear you come in here."

"You look concerned."

She reluctantly nodded. "After seeing this kitchen, I am. No Amish bride would leave it like this. No Amish woman, period, actually."

"It's very much how my mother arranged things." Jake moved to pick up a cookbook from the shelf, and an explosion of dust followed.

"That's what concerns me. Anna should have put her own mark in here by now. Surely there were wedding gifts she could be displaying, recipe books, other things." Mary looked around and then returned her attention to Jake. "But I don't see any of that."

The front door opened, and Caleb stepped back inside, preventing further discussion of the subject. The younger Miller closed the door behind him and paused a moment before joining them in the kitchen.

"Everything all right?" Jake asked him.

Caleb paused again then nodded. "Yes, sure. Everything is fine."

"Julie looked awfully upset," Mary said, though she knew it was none of her business.

He turned his attention to her. "She was, but she was mistaken in what she thought happened. I explained but…" Caleb shrugged. "Well, she has her opinion, and I have my facts. The two do not agree." He turned abruptly to his brother. "So, Jakob, the place looks mostly unchanged from when our parents were here, *ja*?"

"Yes, and frankly, I'm surprised by that."

"And why is that?" Caleb's brows rose. "Are you not glad the traditions have been preserved?"

For a moment, Jake looked conflicted. Then he shook his head. "A bride should have a say in her home, and this is yours and Anna's now. I don't see her touch anywhere. Haven't you let her decorate as she pleases?"

Quick irritation rose on Caleb's face. "What passes between a husband and wife is no one else's business."

A tense moment passed as neither of them spoke. Mary didn't dare interject her opinion, although she agreed whole-heartedly with Jake.

"Right," Jake finally said. "I'm sorry, Caleb. I shouldn't have said that."

Caleb's expression softened. "No, I am the one who should apologize. Anna is very busy with church work and her projects. You warned me that the transition from bachelor to husband would be difficult after all these years alone, and I did not listen. But she is good for me, Jakob, even if she is a bit high strung, and with time she will settle in and be a fine wife. I know this. I just need to give her time."

"I want that for you," Jake said. "You waited a long time for the right woman."

"As did you," he said. "From what you've shared with me, you seemed very happy with Ellen."

"I was." Jake paused as if considering his words. "It was my pride that prevented me from bringing her to visit my Amish family. I knew that my presence here would be awkward for all of you, and I didn't want to subject my family to that. Or Ellen." Jake took a deep breath and let it out slowly. "Anyway, I'm here now, and I don't intend to allow my pride or whatever reaction

I'll get from church members who knew me before I left Bird-in-Hand to drive me away again."

Caleb slapped Jake's back. "I do not think you need to worry about that overly much, Jakob. You were never baptized and thus never shunned. But if any of our friends tell me I cannot spend time with my own bruder..." He frowned, and his face looked like thunder. "Anyone who does not like the fact that Jakob Miller is welcomed in my home will find out quickly that he or she will need to change their tune."

Jake grinned. "So, what are you working on today?"

"Come and see," Caleb said. "It is a cradle."

"Are you in need of one?" Jake asked him.

"Not yet, but a man can hope." He slid Mary a quick glance then nodded toward the door. "I have other things in the works as well, including a few pieces I will be bringing to Secondhand Blessings next week."

"I would love to see those," Mary said. "And the cradle."

They stepped out into the afternoon sunshine and followed the path to the workshop. Caleb opened the door, and the smell of sawdust assailed Mary's nose. It was a familiar scent and a comforting one.

Daddy had loved to do a little woodworking from time to time, and as the youngest, Mary had been his tagalong when he went to the lumber store. She smiled at the memory and followed the men inside.

Caleb led Jake over to a workbench near a bank of east-facing windows and proudly showed off his work on the cradle.

Mary spied an easel in the opposite corner and headed there while the men chatted.

She recognized the design as a French easel meant for transporting canvas, palette, brushes, and paints in its drawer, then unfolding to full size at any location where the painter might wish to do his or her work. Unlike the store-bought models that were made of lightweight beechwood or pine, this beautifully crafted easel had been created from mahogany.

The hinges were brass, and the entire piece had been polished to a glorious sheen. It was as if the easel was a cherished heirloom and not just an artist's tool. Beside the easel was a cardboard box with brushes, tubes of oil paints, and a container of mineral spirits.

She glanced over her shoulder at Caleb and found him watching her. "This is absolutely breathtaking," she told him. "You're very talented, Caleb."

"You are an artist, so I am glad you approve. It is to be a surprise, so do not tell anyone, ja?" He moved toward her. "In fact, I should cover it up," he said, grabbing a lightweight tarp and throwing it over the easel.

"I won't tell anyone. I hope the recipient appreciates it." She paused. "Caleb, I wonder if I could commission you to make one of these easels for me. It wouldn't have to be so grand as this, but I've always wanted a French easel."

"I would be happy to do that," he said. "I could bring it to you at the shop in a few weeks. Is that soon enough?"

Mary beamed. "That would be wonderful. Would you care to give me a peek at what you'll be bringing us next?"

Caleb grinned and motioned for her to join him and Jake for a tour. After a few minutes, Mary sensed that Jake needed some time alone with his brother, so she decided to make an excuse to leave them.

"Do you mind if I go look at the garden, Caleb? It's awfully pretty from here, but I bet it is even prettier up close."

Jake gave her a grateful smile. Later, when they were back in his car, and Caleb was waving goodbye, he slid her a sideways look. "All right. What's your impression?"

"My impression is Caleb is a very talented woodworker, and I'm thrilled that he'll be making an easel for me."

"Not about that." He slowed to a stop at the intersection and then turned to look at her. "About Caleb and Anna. What's your impression of how their marriage is going?"

"Ah, that." She paused to consider her words carefully. "It's hard to say considering Anna wasn't there."

"We talked about that. He said she would be back soon. Then he acted like he wanted us gone before she returned." Jake shrugged. "I let him convince me to go, but now I'm wondering if I did the right thing."

Mary spied a horse and buggy coming over the hill and heading their way. "There's an excuse to go back. I'd recognize Caleb's horse anywhere."

Jake grinned. "Time to meet my sister-in-law."

CHAPTER FIVE

Mary watched the buggy approach and then slow for the turn down the lane leading to the Miller farm. "There are two women in there, Jake. Abigail must be with her. I've never met her."

"But you've seen Anna?"

"Yes. She's been coming to the weekly quilting circle that meets in the shop. She doesn't say much at them though. I don't think she gets much pleasure out of it. My friend Rachel Fischer says Anna's thrown herself into just about every project and meeting their community has going."

"I remember a family of Fischers who lived not far from here. Is she Amish?"

"Rachel?" Mary nodded. "Yes she is."

"Probably married to one of the Fischer boys, then." He made a U-turn and headed toward Caleb's home again.

They arrived back at the farm just in time to see the two women climb down from the buggy while Caleb held the reins.

"You must be Anna," Jake called as he stepped out of the car. "I'm Jakob, Caleb's brother. And I understand you've met Mary."

Mary took note of Jake's use of the Amish version of his name. Then she turned to the petite woman standing beside Caleb and smiled. "Hello, Anna. It's very nice to see you again."

She purposefully made her smile as bright as she could, and Anna, with a quick glance at Caleb, nodded at her. "Yes," she said stiffly. "It is nice to see you again."

Then Anna turned to Jake. "Jakob," she said. "I have heard about you."

"All good, I hope," Jake said, ignoring Caleb's glare to look around then return his attention to Anna. "There was a woman with you. Where did she go?"

"My *schwesder*," Anna said.

"Abigail stays in the dawdy haus," Caleb interjected. "Likely she has gone there. Anna, take our guests inside. I will see to the horse."

Jake glanced at Mary. "I'll help you, Caleb."

Mary looked at Anna. "And I would be happy to help you start dinner while the men are busy."

"Mrs. Yoder sent a pot of stew. Caleb will bring it from the buggy." Anna paused to look over in the direction where the men were walking.

Now that was strange. But it explained the lack of evidence of cooking in the kitchen.

As soon as Caleb and Jake disappeared into the barn, Anna stopped short on the path to the front door and whirled around to stare at Mary. "Why are you here? Do you think I am not capable of being a wife to Caleb?"

The sudden vehemence behind the words stunned Mary into temporary silence. When she recovered, she chose her response carefully. "Jakob is here to see his brother and to meet you. As to what I think, Caleb has told me you are a good wife. I believe him."

Anna's expression immediately softened. She even smiled a little. "He has?"

"Yes."

"His bruder, does he believe that?

"You would have to ask Jakob," Mary said. "I couldn't speak for him. I do know he wants Caleb to be happy."

Anna frowned. "I see no reason to talk to him." She played with the string on her kapp and then looked over toward the barn.

Mary was getting whiplash with Anna's mood changes. "How did you meet Caleb?" she asked.

"*Daed* is a customer of Caleb's. He thought us a good match, and Caleb agreed."

"Did you know Caleb before the wedding?"

"We met once or twice, that is all."

"Well, Caleb is a nice man. I've known him since he was a child." She thought of the cradle under construction in the workshop and of the things Caleb said about his bride. "He seems to be happy with the arrangement."

Once again, Anna smiled and asked, "He said that?"

"Yes," Mary assured her. "And now he'd like you to get to know his brother."

Anna's smile turned once again to a frown, and she stamped her foot. "Take Jakob and go, please."

Again, Anna had stunned Mary with a swift change of attitude. "Have I offended you?"

Anna clenched her fists and put them on her hips. "It is just best if you go. Now."

Rather than give in, Mary shook her head. "I doubt Jakob will agree. He really does want to get to know his brother's wife."

Anna looked up, her brown eyes blazing. "But I do not wish to know him."

"I think you'll change your mind once you spend some time with him." Mary nodded toward the front door. "Let's you and I go inside and make some biscuits to go with that stew."

Anna squinted at her. "Are you really here because of the fire?"

"What fire?" Mary shook her head. "No, I just thought I would help—"

"You are here because of the fire. Go! Just go now." When Mary said nothing, Anna turned toward the barn. "Caleb! Come here!"

"Anna, I meant no harm. I only thought I could help you with—"

"Caleb!"

"Anna, stop. I'm sorry. I didn't mean to upset you. I don't know about a fire. What does that have to do with—"

"Caleb!"

Mary looked toward the barn and spied Caleb and Jake hurrying their way. Swinging from Caleb's hand was a covered cast-iron pot that presumably contained the neighbor's stew.

"What happened?" Caleb asked.

"I don't know," Mary told him. "We were talking, and I asked if I could help. Anna got upset."

When Mary returned her attention to the spot where Anna had stood, she saw that Caleb's wife was gone. Caleb hurried past them to the front door that Anna had left open. Jake moved to follow but stopped short when Caleb turned around to face him.

"What did you say to her?" Jake asked Mary.

Mary shook her head. "I told her we could make biscuits to go with the stew. I thought I was being helpful."

"I am sorry. Please, just go," Caleb said to Jake.

"Caleb," Mary said gently, "I'm the one who's sorry. I don't know what I said, but it was the wrong thing, so please convey my apologies to Anna."

"I am sure whatever you said was fine," he told her.

She thought a moment. "Anna mentioned a fire." At Caleb's stunned look, Mary continued. "What fire?"

He shook his head. "Please forget you heard that."

"But Caleb, I did hear it. And Anna went from calm to upset a couple of times in just the few minutes I stood here. That concerns me."

"Mary, we should go." Jake turned to Caleb. "I'm not leaving town any time soon, but I won't come out here again unless I'm invited. Will you come see me in town? I'm staying at Muhlenberg's."

"I will," Caleb said. "Monday afternoon when I make my deliveries."

Jake embraced his brother. "Let's go," he said to Mary over his shoulder as he stalked toward the car.

"I'm so sorry." She hurried to catch up. "I had no idea I was causing trouble. I was only trying to help."

"So was I," Jake said on an exhale of breath when they were both in the car. "And I'm concerned with Anna's behavior too. I told Caleb as much when we were alone in the barn. He's hoping she'll learn the ways of this community, and that once she settles in she'll be fine."

"I don't know." Mary buckled her seat belt and turned to look at Jake. "She just seems so…"

"Erratic?" he offered. "I saw that indirectly in the weeks before their wedding. First Caleb emailed me with the news that she wanted a small wedding. Then a big wedding. Then no wedding until later in the fall. It just went around and around until a few weeks ago when Caleb informed me the wedding had happened."

"Just like that?" she asked, trying to imagine such a thing.

"Apparently. My sisters were copied on the email. That's how we all found out."

"And you think that was Anna's doing?"

He gave her an even look then turned the key to start the car. "I do. What do you think?"

"I have no idea what to think. She said she and Caleb didn't know each other much before the wedding. Did you know that?"

"Caleb told me Anna was the daughter of one of his customers near Pittsburgh. I had hoped there was a romance and courtship, but given Caleb's age, all those years of being a bachelor, and the distance involved, maybe I was wrong."

Mary tried to imagine a courtship between Caleb and Anna. She'd seen stranger matches work out just fine, but these two were a conundrum.

"Jake, what fire was Anna talking about? She seemed very upset, and all I did was offer to help her make biscuits."

"I have no idea." He looked at his watch. "Speaking of biscuits, what do you say we continue with our dinner plans?"

"Yes, I'm starved." Mary grinned. "I don't suppose you'd be willing to give me a hint where we're going."

"What would you say if I told you we're going to the Smuckers' Cornfield Banquet out on the Old Philadelphia Pike?"

"I'd think you were teasing me," she said.

He gave her a look then turned his attention to driving. She waited for him to say more, but he didn't.

"You're serious." She laughed. "Oh my goodness, Jake. Would you believe that I've never been?"

He slid her a sideways look. "Neither have I. What do you say? Are you in?"

"I'm in," she declared.

True to its name, the banquet was held under open skies in the middle of Mr. Smucker's cornfield and boasted barbecue chicken, potatoes, Pennsylvania Dutch chowchow and, of course, corn—among other things. Dessert was whoopie pies from the Bird-in-Hand Bakery and Café.

Though her sisters proclaimed it a terrible tourist trap, Mary had secretly wanted to go for years. And now here she was.

"I'm glad I'm not the only one who likes to play tourist in Bird-in-Hand," Jake said. "I miss it here sometimes."

She took note of his use of the word *sometimes*. It didn't take a genius to see that the Jakob Miller that baseball had released to the world hadn't returned at all. Jake Miller, the man that skinny kid had become, was only visiting, despite the fact that he told Caleb he'd be around a while.

He parked and then hurried over to open Mary's door for her. "After you," he said as he nodded to the entrance where a stream of tourists was filing in.

Mary fell in line with Jake beside her. A few of the folks around them recognized the former baseball star and asked for pictures or autographs. After the third time Mary was left holding a fan's phone while an infatuated fan posed with him, she could only laugh.

"I see why you needed me here," she said when she'd returned the phone to the grinning teenager. "But you might have warned me that I'd be your own personal paparazzo."

They shared a laugh, and then Jake handed over their tickets and walked her inside the fenced-in area. The first order of business was a hayride. Mary climbed up beside Jake, and they set off laughing like tourists. If anyone on the ride recognized Jake, they didn't let on.

They climbed down off the ride still laughing as they picked the hay off their clothes. A few minutes later they settled at a table in a shady spot with two bottles of water.

"Okay," Jake said. "I've not had the opportunity to ask this, so tell me about you. What's happened since I left?"

"Oh, no. We can talk about all that boring stuff like how I became an Indiana housewife and mother over our corn and coleslaw. I want to hear about how you became famous and pitched a no-hitter in the World Series."

He chuckled. "I'd rather tell you about how I survived medical school and my internship. That was much harder. Baseball? That was fun."

"You always made it look fun," she said. "I often wondered if you would ever realize how good you were. Then that baseball scout showed up at our farm and convinced you to show him what you could do."

Jake's eyes widened. "I was glad he spotted me," he said. "But I wasn't happy I broke your barn in the process."

"The scout was sure impressed," Mary said. "I can't remember whether it was my father or yours who demanded you fix the board though."

"Probably mine," he said. "Daed never did understand my love of baseball, and I know he was disappointed I didn't return to the farm."

"I'm sorry about that. I know it's been hard."

Jake's phone rang before he could respond. He looked down at his phone and then back up at Mary. "It's Caleb. This is the first time he's ever called me. I always call him. Something must be wrong."

"Yes, go ahead. Answer it," Mary told him.

Jake rose and took a few steps away. "Caleb, hey," he said as he lifted the phone to his ear. "Is everything all right?"

Mary watched him closely but tried not to eavesdrop. Jake turned away, and suddenly his head jerked up. Something was wrong.

"What is it?" she asked him when he ended the call. "Has something happened?"

Frantically, Jake shoved his phone back into his pocket and grabbed her hand. "That was Mr. Yoder, Caleb's neighbor. We have to go—now."

"What's happened? Is Caleb all right?"

"No." He pulled her to her feet and toward the car. "There was an explosion at Caleb's.

"The workshop is on fire, and no one knows where he is."

CHAPTER SIX

Jake swerved around the police roadblock at the Miller farm's driveway and gunned the engine to head toward the house. Mary held on tight just as she had been doing ever since they raced out of the Smuckers' and headed for the plume of smoke easily visible in the western sky.

Twilight had descended, and the red and blue lights from the fire truck and emergency responders glared against a purple August sky as they pulled up as close to the buildings as possible.

They'd driven in stony silence. Words weren't necessary. Now, with the horror of the scene unfolding in front of her, words weren't possible.

How could the idyllic farm have become the location of such a nightmare? It made no sense.

Jake threw the car into PARK and turned off the engine then jumped out, leaving his door wide open in the process. Acrid smoke filled the vehicle's interior while the roar of diesel engines competed with the crackle of the fire to drown out all other noises. Mary climbed out to follow Jake.

A police officer whose name tag read STEPHENS stepped between Jake and the fire trucks, but the former athlete merely sidestepped him and continued on. A second policeman pulled his car up behind Jake's rental.

"You can't be here," Stephens called to Mary.

"I don't have much choice." Mary's heart slammed against her chest. "I'm with Caleb's brother, Jake Miller."

"*The* Jake Miller?" the officer asked. "Where'd he go?"

Jake's silhouette was easily spotted among the men dousing water on the flames. He was talking with one of the firefighters and frantically pointing. From her vantage point, Mary could see Amish men and firefighters working together to put out the fire that raged in what was Caleb's workshop just a few hours ago.

"That's him," she managed as her heart wrenched.

"He's with the captain," Stephens said. "But lady, you've got to stay out of the way."

She nodded. "I'll stay right here. Is that okay?"

Stephens's radio crackled. "Unless someone tells you to leave, I guess so."

Mary wrapped her arms around her waist and leaned against the car as Stephens went to speak to the other officer. "Oh Father, help, please!" was all she could manage as she broke down in tears.

Her phone buzzed in her pocket, and Mary retrieved it. Elizabeth. She greeted her sister with, "I'm with Jake at Caleb's farm. There's a fire, and they can't find Caleb."

"I know," Elizabeth said. "John heard it on the radio and called me. Is Anna okay?"

Anna and Abigail. Her heart lurched again. "Oh, Elizabeth, I haven't seen either Anna or her sister. I need to find out where they are. I'll call you back."

She tucked her phone into her pocket and made her way around the car to the police cruiser still parked behind it. The officer inside was talking to someone on his phone.

Tapping on the window, she called to the man inside. "Officer, where is Anna Miller and her sister Abigail? Have they found them?"

He rolled down the window. "Ma'am, you're going to have to let us do our jobs."

"I'm trying to help," she said, now desperate to have him listen to her.

"We're aware there are two women and one man living on this property, and we're doing all we can to ensure their safety. You need to go to a safe place and wait."

Mary turned away. Chaos still reigned all around. She made her way past Jake's car to the path leading to the Miller home. She decided to go around back to the dawdy haus and check it out. It wasn't near the workshop, so it was technically "a safe place." *Easier to ask forgiveness than permission,* she thought.

She looked around to make sure no one was paying attention to her and slipped around the main house. She quickly and quietly entered the little home and found it was comprised of a sitting room, a small kitchenette, and a single bedroom, all tidy and neat, with neither sister in sight. The women must be together, possibly in the main house.

If no one had searched the house, then at least Mary could do that. The firefighters were getting the fire under control, so it wasn't likely to spread to the house now. Likely if Anna was there, she was probably terrified and would rather be found by a friendly face than a stranger, even if Abigail was with her.

Several windows had been shattered, presumably from the explosion, and the interior was dark. Otherwise, the house was untouched by the flames. Mary glanced around and then hurried to the front door and stepped inside.

"Anna?" she called. "Are you here? Abigail?"

She hurried into the kitchen and then turned and went the opposite direction to the bedrooms. Asking herself what she might do if she was afraid, Mary even checked under the beds, but there was no sign of Anna or her sister.

She went back to the bedroom and looked around again. The room was aglow with the red and blue lights of the emergency vehicles parked outside the broken window. The wood floor was sprinkled with glass that shone like carelessly tossed diamonds.

"Anna, Abigail!" Mary called again just in case she'd missed a spot where the women might be hiding. "Anna, if you're here, please come out. We need to know that you're safe. Abigail? Are you here?"

A hand touched her shoulder, and Mary gasped then jumped. She turned around to see John Marks standing there holding a flashlight, his normally immaculate uniform damp and streaked with soot.

His expression told her there was news. And that she was in trouble.

"What is it?" she asked him. "Has something happened? Did you find Anna or Abigail?"

He scowled at her. "You know you shouldn't be in here." Then his eyes lost their sternness, and he looked at the floor. "No, we haven't found the women, but Caleb has been found. Jake is with him." He put his hand on her arm. "Mary, it's not good."

The comment refused to stick. Rather, the words slid away as she tried to make sense of them. "Not good?" Mary shook her head but felt as if she were moving in slow motion. "Is he..."

"Dead?" John supplied in that no-nonsense way he had. "No. The air ambulance is on the way. Jake asked that I tell you he'll be going with Caleb. He left the keys in his car so you can get home."

"Yes. Yes, of course. Thank you. Is there any news of Caleb's condition?"

"He has acute respiratory distress from smoke inhalation, and from what they can tell, second-degree burns on his hands and arms." He paused. "The wife. Do you think she was here with him when the explosion happened? And I understand there's a sister too?"

"Jake and I were with Caleb and Anna just a few hours ago. When we left, Abigail was in the dawdy haus, where she's been staying."

"What was the purpose of your visit with Caleb and Anna?" She shrugged. "Jake had never met Anna."

"So Caleb invited him over here to meet Anna?"

"No, Jake just decided to come out here despite the fact that Anna was reluctant to have him. You know, John, if I didn't know any better, I would think you were interrogating me."

"I'm not interrogating you, Mary. But you are a witness." He gestured to the pocket where he kept his notebook. "I'd write it all down, but my notebook is wet."

"Okay, well, Caleb was glad to see us. When we first got here he was alone. He took both of us on a tour of the workshop. He was so proud of the—"

"Wait," John interrupted. "You and Jake were in the workshop today?"

"This afternoon. Probably around four thirty, give or take." He held up his hand. "Hold on. Let me find someone who can record this. You may have noticed a detail that will help us discover a cause for this fire."

"I don't know, John," she said as he led her back through the house toward the front door. "Everything seemed fine in the workshop."

"No fumes or open flames?"

"Nothing like that," she said. "I'm an artist. I know about flammable paints and cleaners, and there was no indication of anything like that. I did see a container of mineral spirits, but it was capped and not in a precarious position or near any heat source. Jake and I went inside with Caleb, and then Julie Bettencourt arrived." Mary's heartrate accelerated, and she gasped. "John, Caleb went out to speak with her, and Jake and I stayed inside. They argued, and we both heard her say she could burn his business down with him inside it. You don't think—"

"We won't know what to think until we ask a lot more questions," John said firmly. "We're not going to jump to conclusions, Mary. No matter what you heard."

Once outside, Mary followed John to his patrol car. "Have a seat inside while I find someone to take your statement," he said.

The chop of helicopter blades cut through the roar of the fire trucks' engines and the shouts of first responders. It was almost dark now, so the lights of the aircraft were easily visible as it neared the farm.

Mary searched the crowd for signs of Jake and Caleb. Everywhere she looked were firefighters and policemen going about their duties alongside neighbors who had come to offer their help.

"Mary!"

She followed the sound of Jake's voice to see him walking toward her. His clothes and face were streaked with soot, and there were smears of what looked like blood on his sleeves.

He walked like a man unaware of his surroundings, his eyes focused only on her. She hurried to meet him. "How is Caleb?" she demanded.

"Alive," Jake told her. "Thank God, he's alive."

"And Anna?" she asked. "Did anyone find her or Abigail?"

"Not that I know of," he said. "I'm going with Caleb."

"Yes, he needs you right now. I'm going to give a statement once John finds someone to take it. He said you were leaving me your car. I'll get it to you as soon as I know where they'll be taking Caleb."

His expression told her he'd heard, but his eyes were focused on the helicopter that was landing in the pasture. "I'm not worried about the car, but I have to go. Just pray, please. Caleb is alive, and that's by God's grace alone. Keeping him that way is going to take another miracle."

She reached to touch his sleeve. Words failed, so she managed a nod and then took a step backward.

"I'll text you when we get to the hospital," he told her.

Then he was gone. Mary stood close enough to watch as a gurney carrying Caleb was loaded onto the air ambulance.

Jake climbed inside, and the doors closed. A moment later, the helicopter lifted and slowly disappeared out of sight.

The first responders went back to their work, but Mary could only stare in the direction where the two Miller brothers were headed as she whispered prayers to the One who could make everything better.

By the time she finished speaking with the policeman who recorded her statement, Mary got a text from Jake telling her that Caleb was in critical care at Lancaster General but would likely be transferred to a larger facility once he stabilized.

If he stabilized.

GET SOME SLEEP AND I'LL UPDATE YOU TOMORROW.

I'M COMING THERE TONIGHT UNLESS YOU DON'T WANT COMPANY, she texted as she walked over to Jake's car. She hit SEND and climbed behind the wheel.

There was a long pause. I COULD USE THE COMPANY. THANKS.

CAN I BRING ANYTHING?

JUST YOURSELF.

After a brief stop at home, Mary headed for Lancaster General where she found Jake seated alone in the ICU waiting room. He managed a smile when he saw her.

Her smile was slower in coming. Poor Jake looked a fright, and his expression told her he was completely worn out and more than a little worried for his younger brother.

She quietly sat down next to him and patted his arm. Once again, words were not necessary.

"Have they found Anna or her sister?" he asked after a while.

Mary shook her head. "I gave a statement to one of the officers on the scene. They know Anna and Abigail were on the property when we left this afternoon."

Jake took her hand and held on, and Mary knew there were no words she could say to help him.

With the sounds of bells and alarms from distant hospital rooms sounding in the background and hospital staff and visitors coming and going, somehow the night passed, and daylight peered through the waiting room window.

CHAPTER SEVEN

T he morning after the fire was a Sunday, and according to the pastor, churches all across the area were lifting up prayers for Caleb Miller. No bodies had been found, so Anna Miller and her sister were tentatively declared as missing.

With the daylight came the realization that the workshop was a total loss. There was enough left for the arson team to sift for clues as to what caused the fire, and that was the scene that greeted Elizabeth when she drove onto the property after church.

She had skipped Sunday dinner. Without Mary there, and given the situation with Caleb, neither she nor Martha felt up to it. Still, armed with the knowledge that Anna was still out there somewhere—her sister too—Elizabeth determined to do a little investigating of her own.

John had warned Elizabeth that the investigators might have the scene roped off to the point where she wouldn't be able to get onto the property. Fortunately, she got as far as the deep ruts left in the dirt road by the fire trucks before she was stopped by a uniformed East Lampeter police officer with a badge that indicated she was Ruth Hayford.

"Can I help you, ma'am?" she asked when Elizabeth rolled down the window.

"I'm looking for Anna Miller and her sister. Have they been found?"

"I'm sorry. I can't comment on an ongoing investigation."

"Would you mind if I took a look around, then? Anna and I are friends from quilting circle, and I feel so helpless not knowing. ...." She glanced over at the ruins and then back at Officer Hayford.

The officer seemed to be studying Elizabeth. "You're John Marks's friend, aren't you?"

"I am," she said.

Another moment of studying her, and the policewoman nodded. "All right, look. I'll let you in, but you can't go into the workshop or past anything marked with crime scene tape. Deal?"

Elizabeth nodded. "Deal. And thank you."

Elizabeth rolled up her window and drove around the crime scene tape to follow the driveway past the house and the barn to stop at the dawdy haus.

She knocked, and the door slipped open. "Abigail?" Elizabeth called. "Are you here? It's Elizabeth Classen."

Peering into the shadowed space, she could see no one. Behind her there was no sign of the police officer or any of the arson investigators. Not that they could have seen her out here without traveling around the barn and house.

"I'm coming in," she called as she opened the door wider and then stepped inside. From her vantage point she could see all the way into a tiny kitchen and adjoining sitting area.

She closed the door and then turned around to consider her next move. "Anyone here?" she tried once again.

Silence.

"Okay, time to investigate, though I have no idea what I'm looking for."

By taking a few steps to the right, she was able to look into a cozy and simply furnished bedroom. Just inside the bedroom door was a single unmade bed that might have been covered by a quilt. It was difficult to see exactly, due to the pile of clothing that covered it.

Englisch clothes, as the Amish would call them.

Elizabeth lifted a pair of very modern-looking women's jeans that had been crumpled beneath a stack of T-shirts bearing logos for popular bands and fashion brands. The remainder of the garments were of a similar style, all modern and all definitely not belonging to an Amish woman. Wasn't Abigail as committed to the Amish church as Anna seemed to be?

Elizabeth's phone rang, and she jumped. She tugged it out of her pocket. It was John.

With fumbling fingers and her heart racing, she managed to answer the call. "John? Is everything all right? Has something happened to Caleb?"

"They found Anna."

Elizabeth gripped the phone. "Where was she?"

"At the bus station in Lancaster." He paused. "She was taken in for questioning."

"Was Abigail with her?"

"The report doesn't mention her, but it's possible she was detained and then released. I'll know more once I speak to the officers on scene." He was quiet for a moment. "But there's more."

"What else?"

"There's been another fire reported. Crews are on the scene, and the blaze is under control."

"Oh no," she said under her breath.

"Owner told officers that he and Caleb had a disagreement just a few days before the incident. No details yet on what sort of disagreement, but the fact that there's a connection to Caleb Miller raises a flag, as does the fact that the business is Amish owned. The fellow's name is Hershberger. Isaiah Hershberger."

"Oh no," she said again. "Isaiah owns a print and sign shop. He's done some work for our shop. That's probably what he did for Caleb too. Is he all right?"

"I believe he's one of the men who suffered smoke inhalation. Apparently he stayed in the building until he was certain the attached family quarters was cleared of people."

"How did the fire start?" she asked as she made her way back toward the front door and stepped out into the warm August afternoon.

"In a dumpster beside the building."

She let out a long breath. "Like the one at Amos Mast's place. But Anna was at the bus station, so she couldn't have started it."

"She definitely could have. Hershberger Print and Sign is in Lancaster. Near the bus station. And it gets worse. There was a church service going on in the family quarters at the back of the building when the fire started."

"That's terrible, John. Was anyone hurt?"

"Initial report is two with injuries and three with suspected smoke inhalation. They're on their way to Lancaster General right now." He paused. "You know what that means, right?"

"That others were hurt," she said. "Yes, that's terrible."

"It is, but that's not what I was referring to. This fire was set while church services were being held. That makes the fire a possible arson on a church building, which is a federal crime." He paused again. "It's not just our local task force now. The Feds will be involved."

CHAPTER EIGHT

Mary tried to blend into the background as the detectives spoke with Jake. There were two of them, one graying at the temples and the other young with close-cropped blond hair. They had appeared in the ICU waiting room just minutes after Mary returned from looking for a muffin and coffee. The only other visitors to the ICU had left at daybreak to get some sleep, so it was just she and Jake sitting in the hard, plastic chairs, anxious for the top of the hour when Jake could slip in and see Caleb again.

A flash of badges, and the pair had Jake's attention. "I'm Ken Bennett," the older man said. "This is my partner, Abe Simon. We'd like to ask some questions about what happened yesterday at the Miller farm."

"Yes, of course," Jake said. "This is Mary Baxter. She's an old friend who was with me at the farm yesterday. She can answer most of the same questions I can."

"Most?" the younger officer asked.

"We weren't together the entire time," Jake explained. "At one point I was with Caleb, and Mary was with Anna."

A look passed between the detectives. "Just you, please," Detective Bennett said. "Will you excuse us, Ms. Baxter?"

"Yes, of course."

Mary would excuse them, but she certainly wouldn't be let-ting them out of her sight. And she'd be listening if she could manage it.

Jake walked with them over to the corner where the hospi-tal auxiliary kept the industrial-sized coffeepots. Not too far away, and yet the illusion of privacy was created.

But Mary could hear them. She was careful, though, to look as if she could not. As if she was still reading yesterday's newspaper that someone had tossed aside.

If they noticed her, they might move farther away. The men had seemed furtive when they arrived in the ICU waiting room, and it was clear their words were meant only for Jake.

"She's agreed to give her statement," Mary heard Detective Simon say. "The officer on the scene said her claim is that she was returning to her parents' home when she was picked up at the bus station. She had a ticket to Pittsburgh on her."

"I see." Jake made eye contact with Mary then quickly returned his attention to the detectives. "So are you telling me Anna is a suspect?"

"I'm not saying that," Bennett said. "We're just gathering facts right now." He paused. "I'm not going to sugarcoat this, Mr. Miller. If your brother lives, and Anna is responsible for his injuries, she's looking at a number of charges starting with arson if she's the one who did it. Which is still to be deter-mined. We're also looking for the Bettencourt woman, but she's not answering her door and isn't at her office."

"And if Caleb doesn't survive?" Jake asked tersely.

"Murder," Simon told him. "I take it you didn't know Julie Bettencourt before you heard her argue with your brother."

"Never met the woman," he said. "At least not that I can remember. I vaguely recall her husband having some business related to supplying lumber to furniture shops, but I may be wrong about that. I haven't been back in Bird-in-Hand in decades."

"Okay. Tell me about Anna's sister." Detective Simon retrieved his notebook from his shirt pocket and flipped the pages until he found what he was looking for. Bennett did the same.

"Here it is," Simon said. "Tell me about Abigail Byler, older sister of Anna Miller."

"Not much to tell," Jake said. "Like you said, she's the older sister. Apparently she's lived in the dawdy haus since Caleb and Anna were married, but I only know that because Caleb told me. He said it was something about helping Anna make the transition from her family home to his." He shrugged. "I haven't had a single conversation with her and have only seen her in person once, and that was brief. Basically the time it took for the buggy to pass me."

"But she was at the farm at the same time you were yesterday?"

Jake told them about seeing Abigail and Anna together in Caleb's buggy then Abigail disappearing before they could meet her.

Detective Simon made a note. "Is it possible that she left the farm after you saw her?"

"Anything is possible," Jake told them. "I was focused on my brother and his new wife." He looked at the floor. "I haven't been home in a long time, and I wanted to get to know my brother again."

"What made you decide now was the time to do that?" Bennett asked.

"I told you, I wanted to meet his new wife." He sighed. "A while back I got to thinking about how close Caleb and I used to be. So I found his business online, sent him an email, and told him I'd like to stay in touch."

"And that got a reaction?"

"That and the fact that I told him he ought to use birch instead of maple for the rockers he makes." Jake chuckled. "Caleb never did like being told what to do, but later I noticed he had added birch rockers to his online catalog."

The trio shared a smile. Then Jake sobered.

"From there we developed a friendship again. We sent emails back and forth, sometimes three and four a day. Just talking about our days, what Caleb was working on, how things were for me in New York. You know. Just things brothers would talk about." Jake paused to shake his head. "Caleb followed me around like a shadow when he was a kid. We were once so close, and I was determined not to lose him again."

"Not even to a wife?" Simon asked.

Mary saw Jake flush. "What are you insinuating?" he asked harshly.

"Nothing." The young officer responded with a shrug. "Just asking questions."

"How long ago was it that you sent that email that revived your relationship with your brother, Mr. Miller?" Bennett shifted positions. "Approximately. And was Anna Byler in the picture at that time?"

"Nearly two years ago," Jake told him, traces of anger still showing in his expression. "And no, she was not. Caleb was a confirmed bachelor. He said it suited him."

"Did you think so?"

"That it suited him?" Jake shook his head. "No, but that was Caleb. He was always determined to do what he was going to do, so there wasn't much anyone could say to the contrary when he declared himself a lifelong bachelor."

Detective Bennett's phone rang, and he looked down to check it. "I need to take this," he said to Simon then stepped away.

"So you were surprised when he announced his engagement to the woman he ended up marrying?"

"By then I wasn't. He might claim it suited him, but I hated to think of him all alone in that big house without a family of his own. I encouraged him to be open to the possibility that God might have a different plan for him, even at his age."

Jake paused and looked away. For a long time he said nothing. Mary slid another glance in his direction and caught him wiping his eyes with the back of his hand.

Bennett stepped back toward the men. "Mr. Miller, do you know a man by the name of Isaiah Hershberger?"

"No," Jake said. "Should I?"

"Not necessarily." Bennett nodded to Simon. "I'll brief you in a minute. Do you have any more questions for Mr. Miller?"

A door opened behind Jake, and a nurse stepped into the waiting room. "Mr. Miller? The doctor would like to speak with you."

Jake looked first at Simon and then at Bennett. "Are we done here, or do you want to wait until I've spoken with Caleb's doctor?"

"I think we're done," Bennett said though Simon appeared disappointed at the statement.

Finally the younger detective nodded and folded up his notebook to put it away. "Yeah, we're done, but stick around Bird-in-Hand in case we need to ask more questions, okay?"

He gave the two men an even look. "I'm not going anywhere until I know my brother is on the mend and the person who put him in the hospital is caught." Jake's expression softened. "He needs me, and I'll stay until he doesn't. Now if we're done here…"

"Yes, for now." Simon handed him a card. "Call me if you think of anything else that might be helpful. We are committed to catching whoever did this to your brother."

Jake shook hands with both detectives and then disappeared through the ICU door with the nurse. As if on cue, both men turned to face Mary.

Rather than look away, she met their gazes and stood. "I was interviewed last night at the farm," she told them. "But I'm happy to answer any questions you have. This person needs to be caught."

"How did you first meet Caleb?" Simon asked her.

Mary walked a few steps toward them. "That goes way back. We both grew up here. But then we lost touch after Jake went off to play baseball and I married my husband and moved away. When I returned to Bird-in-Hand and reopened my parents' store, Secondhand Blessings, with my sisters, Caleb became one of our suppliers."

"So you knew him on a professional level only?" Bennett asked.

"Yes," she said. "Other than brief conversations when he was delivering his pieces, I didn't really speak with him."

The men exchanged a look. Then Bennett let out a long breath. "And the wife or her sister? Any interaction with her?"

"Anna has come to the Thursday quilting circle at the store a few times, so I've met her and exchanged polite conversation, but nothing else. My sister, Elizabeth, knows her slightly better because she also attends the quilting circle."

Mary's phone buzzed in her pocket. "Excuse me, please."

She pulled out the phone and saw the call was from a number she didn't recognize. Pressing IGNORE, she returned the phone to her pocket. "Sorry about that. Where were we?"

"You were telling us about Anna Miller," Simon said. "I was about to ask if you had any closer connection to her sister, Abigail Byler."

"I've never spoken to Abigail," she said. "I saw her in the buggy with Anna yesterday, but that's it. I found out yesterday she's living in the dawdy haus at Caleb's."

Bennett nodded. "Everyone's saying the same thing about these two sisters. Is there anyone who knew them well?"

Mary thought a moment. "Mrs. Yoder might. Anna and Abigail were returning from a visit to the Yoder farm when we saw them last night."

"Yoder?" Detective Simon asked. "Do you have a first name for her?"

"She's Bess, and her husband is Benjamin. They're Caleb's neighbors." She paused. "I can give you directions if you need them."

"Considering the number of Yoders in this county, that would be helpful," he said. "One more question, and it doesn't have anything to do with Mrs. Miller or her sister. Yesterday when you and Mr. Miller were driving back to the farm, did you see anything or anyone that stood out? Anything unusual?"

No one had asked her that question. Mary tried to remember the drive to the farm, but all she could recollect was Jake's white-knuckle driving and the way her heart lurched when she saw the workshop in flames.

Had there been other cars on the road? Maybe. Most of the time her eyes had been closed in prayer anyway.

"I'm sorry," she finally told him. "I just can't remember anything that stands out. When we got the news, the only thing both of us could think of was getting there as quickly as we could."

"Julie Bettencourt," Detective Simon said. "Tell me about her."

"About Julie?" Mary shrugged. "She took over for her husband in the family business after he died, and she's worked hard to keep it running. She's also a very nice woman, which makes what Jake and I heard her say all the more shocking."

"And that was?" Simon asked.

Mary repeated what she and Jake heard on Saturday and described Julie's demeanor. "Caleb said it was all just a misunderstanding and didn't seem bothered by it."

"But you were?"

"Not as much at the time as I am now considering that what Julie threatened actually happened."

"Just one more name I want to throw at you," Bennett said. "Isaiah Hershberger. Do you know him?"

"The man who owns the sign shop in Lancaster? Yes, he's done some work for Secondhand Blessings. Why?"

"Something happened this morning. Could turn this entire investigation into a federal case. Then we'd be stepping back and letting the Feds take over."

Detective Bennett nodded to his companion. "In the meantime, Simon and I will get out of your hair. If you think of anything else, will you give us a call?"

"Yes, of course," she said as she accepted a business card from Detective Simon. "But I do have a question for you."

"Sure," he said. "What is it?"

"How long will you keep Anna for questioning?"

"Not long," Bennett said. "She's not under arrest. We'll need to work fast to build a case, or we'll run out of time and have to let her go, especially in light of the allegations against Julie Bettencourt that you and Mr. Miller have made. If the Feds take over, then there's a whole different time line though."

"I haven't made any allegations against Julie," she protested. "I just told you what I heard. There could be a reasonable explanation for what she said."

Simon gave her an incredulous look. "Like what?"

She frowned. "I have no idea," she finally conceded, "but surely there is. She's just such a nice woman."

"Sometimes nice women do things they regret," Simon said. "But we're looking at all angles. We took the wife in because we caught her at the bus station. We might need to have a judge declare her a flight risk. If we find out that Mrs. Bettencourt has tried to make a run for it, we might have to do the same for her."

"What about Anna's sister? Is she being held too?"

"Abigail?" Simon shook his head. "We haven't found her yet, but when we do we'll just want to question her. There's no motive for Abigail that we can figure, at least for now. Unless you know about one we haven't come up with?"

"Me?" Mary shook her head. "Like I said, I don't know Abigail, so I wouldn't have a clue. One more question: Why are you asking me about Isaiah? Is he a suspect?"

"Code blue," echoed through the ICU waiting room, and Mary's breath froze. They'd heard this announcement twice already since she and Jake began their vigil at Lancaster General. Each time, she prayed it wasn't Caleb whose life was hanging in the balance.

"Should we wait, Bennett?" Simon asked his partner.

"To see if that's our guy?" He shook his head. "Let's not. We'll get a call if it is." He looked over at Mary. "I hope it isn't."

CHAPTER NINE

Martha turned off the stand mixer and stepped away from the cookies she'd been attempting to make. For the second time, she'd screwed up the recipe somehow. Too much flour this time.

At least she caught this batch before she baked them.

She lifted the bowl from its place on the stand and walked over to the trash can, where she dumped its ruined contents. This time, instead of marching to the sink to wash the bowl and begin again, she gave up, poured a cup of coffee, and walked into the office with two dogs and a cat following behind her.

Baking could wait.

Martha opened the email program on her computer, and the familiar ding told her she had new emails waiting. Sorting through the store advertisements and junk mail, she arrived at one from Catherine Randall.

The name sounded familiar. Perhaps a friend of Elizabeth's? But what would she be doing sending Martha an email?

She clicked on the envelope icon, and the email opened.

Dear Martha, I hope by now that Elizabeth told you about our conversation at the coffee shop in which I told her I have a friend who is looking to sell exactly the kind of facility that you would need to open your own bakery. I haven't heard from you, so perhaps she forgot?

If so, here are the basics: My friend is looking to sell an established business, and her employees would be willing to stay if you wanted them to. It needs work, but my friend is willing to come down on the price to balance that out. With a little bit of imagination, you could do so much! A storefront for sure, and maybe even catering. The sky's the limit. This is a much-loved endeavor, and my friend is only selling due to health issues.

Let me know if you're interested, and I'll make the introductions. Don't wait too long. This is a once-in-a-lifetime opportunity, and the price is a steal.

Beneath Catherine's signature was her phone number.

Martha glanced up at the clock. Half past four. Too late to interrupt Sunday lunch, and too early to interrupt Sunday dinner. She reached for her phone.

Then her hand froze. What was she thinking?

She had plenty to do right here at Secondhand Blessings without adding to her list of responsibilities. Making the move from baking for the store to actually owning a store that served only her baked goods was a huge step.

A huge responsibility.

A huge dream.

Martha pushed the phone away and sat back in her chair. No. She was too old to start yet another endeavor. Too...

She sighed. Too what? Too afraid?

"Of what?" she asked, causing the menagerie of pets to open their eyes and stare at her. "How can I be afraid when I don't know the details?"

Before she could change her mind, Martha picked up her phone and made the call to Catherine Randall. Catherine gave her all the details she could supply then promised to have her friend call to answer any further questions.

"I'm so excited for you," Catherine said. "You're going to love owning your own shop. It's hard work, but there's just nothing better at the end of the day than seeing the fruits of your labor and knowing you did it. You went for the dream."

A dream she'd never dared to dream. And yet now, perhaps, she could.

Her phone beeped, indicating another call. "I'm sorry, but I've got another call I need to take," she told Catherine. "Thank you for thinking of me. I'll look forward to speaking with your friend soon."

She pressed the button to answer the second call. "Mary? Tell me everything."

"I only have a second to talk," her sister said. "Please pray. Call everyone you know and tell them that prayers are needed for Caleb. He coded."

"Oh no," Martha said as she gripped the phone tighter.

"Doctors are working on him now. That's all I know. Jake went back in, and so far they haven't kicked him out." She paused. "Wait, he's coming out."

Martha could hear a conversation between Mary and Jake but couldn't understand what they were saying. Then Mary returned. "Okay, Caleb is back with us. The doctors are still in with him, and Jake said it was a close call. So keep praying." She paused again. "Hold on."

Another conversation between Mary and Jake. Then Mary returned. "If you're not busy, do you think you could come give me a ride home? Jake is going to try to use his doctor's credentials to be able to stay in the room with Caleb, so it makes no sense for me to sit out here alone. I could drive Jake's car, but that leaves him here without one."

"Sure," Martha said. "I'll grab my keys and come get you."

"Oh, wait," Mary said. "I think a ride just walked in. If Elizabeth is there, I would like to get together with you both and talk about what's happened. Pretty soon the case could be in the hands of federal agents, and we won't hear anything about it anymore."

"Federal agents? Why would they be taking over?" Martha asked.

"Something about an incident at Isaiah Hershberger's store. Is Elizabeth home?"

"No, she went for a drive after church. I'll call her. See you soon."

Martha ended the call. What else could happen today?

"See you soon," Mary echoed as she hung up the phone and slid it into her pocket then turned her attention to Bill. "Hey there," she said to him. "What are you doing here?"

Bill stood with his hands in his pockets and seemed uncomfortable being there. Not that anyone would be comfortable in an ICU waiting room.

"I came to see about Caleb," he told her. "And to check on you. Word got out that you were in a police car at the fire on the Miller property yesterday. I was worried, so I called John. And here you are just like he told me you probably would be. Not in jail."

"No," she said. "I'm not in jail. And I was in the police car because I was giving my statement about what Jake and I saw go on between Caleb and the other people who were there yesterday afternoon."

He looked around then returned his gaze to Mary. "Is Jake here?"

"He's in with Caleb," she said. "There was an incident. He coded." She told him the rest of the details quickly and then added, "So Jake is going to try to use his credentials to stay as close to his brother as he can until he's out of danger. Which leaves me in a bit of a bind."

Bill frowned. "What sort of bind? And how can I help?"

Mary's heart warmed. What a sweet man. The minute she mentioned a problem, he wanted to help. To be the solution. Indeed, he was a good friend.

"Jake came here with Caleb on the air ambulance, so I drove his car. But if I take the car now, Jake will be without one when he's ready to leave." She paused. "And since he's going to be back there with Caleb, there's no need for me to keep him company out here in the waiting room."

A grin rose on Bill's face. "That's not a problem at all, Mary. I'd be happy to be your chauffeur."

Mary picked up her purse and matched his grin. "You are a lifesaver, Bill. Thank you."

They walked together to the elevator. After punching the down button, Bill nodded to the clock on the wall between the sets of elevator doors. "Looks like it's almost suppertime. How about I feed you before I drop you off? I bet you haven't had any kind of decent food since you got here."

Her stomach growled at the thought of actual food. Their dinner at the Smuckers' had been interrupted, and since lunch yesterday she'd only had coffee and a few bites of a strawberry-covered muffin that a hospital auxiliary volunteer insisted she try.

"Maybe a quick bite," she said. "I'll just let Martha know what we're up to so she won't tell Elizabeth to hurry to meet me at home."

The elevator doors opened and then closed again once they were inside. "Sounds like you three Classen women are planning a confab," Bill said.

"We are, or rather I am. I want to talk to them about…" The doors opened to admit a young couple and then closed again. "About some things," she continued, content to leave her answer at that until she and Bill were alone.

"Are you ladies working on solving another mystery?" Bill asked as they were in his car and leaving the hospital parking lot.

"I think so." She paused. "Someone is setting fires, and I think my sisters and I may have a better chance to find out who it is."

"Better than who?" Bill signaled to turn on to the main road. "The police? How could that be? I heard there's a task force they've put together to try to get to the bottom of the case."

Mary chuckled. "I don't mean we're smarter or more equipped than the police. But you know as well as I do, the Amish will be less likely to cooperate with the police than they are with us. They'll talk to us when they might not talk to the police. Plus we know the victims of this arsonist personally. I want to see that person caught before anyone else is hurt or, worse, before someone dies." Mary paused. "Like Caleb almost did today."

Tears rose, and she couldn't help but shed them. Whether it was exhaustion, hunger, or the fact that a man she'd spent time with admiring a cradle and talking about his future was fighting for his life in the intensive care unit, she couldn't stop herself from crying.

And crying.

Bill pulled over in the parking lot of the Burger Barn and swiveled to face her. "Mary, are you all right?" he asked as he yanked his handkerchief out of his pocket and handed it to her. "It's clean. I promise."

Despite her sobs, she managed the beginnings of a smile. "Thank you. You always know what to do, Bill. What would I do without you?"

He sat very still and quiet for a moment, then he reached out to gather her into his arms. "I hope you don't have to find out, Mary."

"Me neither," she managed as she cried on his shoulder. "You're a good friend."

"That's what I want to be," he said as he gently patted her back. "A good friend."

They sat like that until she finally managed to get her emotions under control. Then Mary lifted her head, dried her eyes with Bill's handkerchief, and blew her nose.

"I'll wash this before I return it."

He made a face then grinned. "Sure thing. I owe you some picture frames anyway. I'll trade you my handkerchief for your frames when they're ready." He looked down at her hand and made another face. "And when that's clean."

Mary laughed. "Since we're here at the Burger Barn, how about I treat you to a burger?"

"That's awfully kind of you, Mary, but it's me who's going to treat you. I'm the one who asked you to dinner, and I'm the one who will pay for it." He shrugged. "You can pay next time."

She gave him a sideways look and then tucked the handkerchief in her purse. Bill always made her end up smiling no matter how low she was feeling. He truly was a good friend.

"It's a deal. Now hurry up, and let's get inside. I'm starving."

After ordering, they seated themselves at a booth next to the window. The food arrived a short while later, reminding Mary again how hungry she truly was.

"I haven't been here in years," she told Bill as she dipped a fry in ketchup. "I've forgotten how good it is." She looked over at her companion, but he wasn't eating. "Is something wrong? Isn't that what you ordered?"

He sat back and gave her a look that she couldn't quite decipher. "The order is right, but I'm wondering something, and I need to ask it now before I do anything else."

Mary dipped another french fry. "Okay. Ask away."

"Is there anything going on between you and Jake Miller?"

"Going on?" She shook her head and laughed. "Between me and Jake? You're joking, right?"

But he wasn't. The expression on his face made that clear. Mary sobered. "You're serious. Okay. Well, no. And yes." She paused to let him stew on that answer. "No, there isn't anything romantic going on between Jake and me. There never was, even back when we were teenagers. We were friends. And yes, as I said, if you're asking about friendship, what's going on between me and Jake is that we're friends."

"Like you and me," he said.

She shook her head. "Nope." At his crestfallen look, Mary hurried to continue. "Bill, I hardly know Jake anymore. I just saw him for the first time in more decades than I care to admit yesterday. He's had a rough twenty-four hours, and so have I, and I didn't want him to sit in the waiting room alone, so I stuck around with him. But you? Goodness, I can't name another friend I'd rather spend time with than you. Now if you don't have any more questions, can we please eat our meal?"

Bill grinned and gave her a mock salute. "As you wish."

An hour later, Mary arrived back home to find both Elizabeth and Martha there. "Good," she said as she tossed her purse on the chair and hurried into the kitchen, where her sisters were waiting. "I have so much to tell you."

"I've got news too," Elizabeth said. She placed a teacup in front of Mary and pushed the tea tray close enough for her to choose a tea bag, then she poured the water over it in the cup.

"Well, as long as we're sharing, I have some news as well," Martha told them.

CHAPTER TEN

L et's let Mary tell her news first," Martha said.

Elizabeth nodded. "Yes, go ahead, Mary."

Grateful for her sisters' thoughtfulness, Mary told them what she'd learned about Anna, Abigail, Julie, and the fire at the Hershberger business. She described the detectives and their questions then paused. "So the task force will be subordinate to the federal agents. At least that's how it was explained to me."

"John told me something similar," Elizabeth said. "I worry that the Amish people might shy away from speaking with government agents. They're barely cooperative with local law enforcement as it is, so I can't imagine that they'd agree to talk to federal agents."

"Exactly," Mary agreed. "But they might talk to us. And failing that, they'll talk to Rachel, and she'll talk to us."

"Yes, that's true. And now for my news. I paid a visit to the Miller farm today," Elizabeth told them. "I was out driving and praying for Caleb and thought I would just see what I could do to help."

"They let you just drive in?" Martha asked. "I thought the whole place was a crime scene."

"Some of it is, but I was able to get into the dawdy haus and look around. I thought maybe I could pick up some clues about where Anna and Abigail had gone."

"Did you find anything?" Mary asked. "As far as I know, they still haven't found Abigail."

"Sort of," she said. "In the bedroom was a stack of clothes that were definitely not Amish. There were jeans and tops that an Englischer would wear all thrown on top of the bed."

"Those things weren't there when I went in last night," Mary said. "I walked through the dawdy haus looking for the sisters. Did you tell John what you found?"

Elizabeth seemed to be thinking for a minute. "No, I don't think I did. He called me while I was there and told me that they found Anna at the bus station. He told me about the Hershberger fire, and I forgot all about the clothes."

Mary frowned. "So in between yesterday evening when I went into the dawdy haus and this afternoon when you went in, someone dumped Englisch clothes on the bed?"

"It appears so," Elizabeth replied.

"Okay," Mary said, "I think we need to investigate where those clothes came from. I would assume that if Anna was going back to her parents' house she would have taken her clothes with her. What we don't know is if she took some of them and those are the ones she left?" She looked at Elizabeth. "Did you see a suitcase anywhere in the dawdy haus?"

"No, but then I wasn't looking either," said Elizabeth. "So it's possible there might have been one there." She paused. "If Anna planned her escape, she would want to look different. And the clothes I saw were definitely different."

Martha held up her hand. "But Anna wasn't staying at the dawdy haus," she argued. "Abigail was. How do you know they weren't her clothes?"

Elizabeth looked at her in surprise. "You're right about that, Martha." She shook her head. "But now that I think about it, the jeans looked like they'd be more Anna's size than Abigail's."

Mary pursed her lips. "Let's table that discussion for just a minute and talk about Julie Bettencourt. I know what I heard yesterday, and I know what I saw. But I can't reconcile either of those things with the person I know Julie to be."

"What's this about Julie?" Elizabeth asked. "I just saw her yesterday too. She was at Un-Common Grounds having coffee with a friend. But she didn't stay. She went through the line, ordered her coffee, and then she stopped by our table to speak to us. After that, she said a quick word to her friend and then left in a hurry."

"What time was that?" Mary asked.

"I don't know. Midafternoon, maybe." Elizabeth shrugged. "If I had to guess I'd say sometime around three-ish."

"What did you talk about? It sounds like something in that conversation might have struck a nerve," Martha said.

"Julie asked John if someone would be obligated to report another person's crime to the police if they knew one had been committed. She was careful to speak in generalities and to say her question was purely hypothetical." Elizabeth paused. "But given the expression on her face after John responded, she certainly didn't like the answer."

Martha shook her head. "So let's think about this. Julie may have information about a crime that was committed, and when she saw you having coffee with a police officer, she decided to find out if she was supposed to give up that information or keep quiet about it."

"Yes," Elizabeth said. "We both figured she was hiding something."

"Like information on who was setting fires?" Martha asked.

Elizabeth nodded then looked over at Mary. "But why go to Caleb with that? Was she accusing him of being the arsonist?"

"I don't think so." Mary shifted positions and reached for her cup of tea. "That wasn't the allegation Jake and I heard her make." She repeated the words Julie used. "It sounded like she was furious at Caleb."

"Okay, let's think about *this*, then," Martha said. "From what you heard Julie say to Caleb, we could think that she was about to do something to him, and she was asking John that question in relation to herself—she was afraid someone knew she was about to commit a crime. But what if she knew about a crime someone else was going to commit against Caleb, and she was coming to tell him that before she went to the police? You said that by the time Julie left it seemed that Caleb had calmed her down. Then when he came inside he said she was mistaken in what she thought happened."

The kitchen fell silent. Finally Mary spoke up. "Where is Julie now, though? Let's say she did want to tell Caleb something. Maybe she wanted to warn him about something she'd heard. Why disappear?"

"Has she disappeared?" Martha asked.

Elizabeth shrugged. "John said officers have gone to her house and business, and she wasn't at either place. So yes, it appears she has. And that in itself is suspicious. When you add in what Mary and Jake saw..."

"What they heard wasn't suspicious," Martha argued. "She was talking to Caleb as if he was the one who had started fires and so he deserved to have his business burned down. Why would she warn him if she was going to burn down his workshop?"

Elizabeth held up her hand. "At any rate, we need to find Julie and hear from her what she and Caleb talked about." She looked over at Mary. "Do you think it's too late to drive out there?"

Mary looked out the window, where the sun still shone. The days were longer in August, but there had been little sleep last night. Only what she could grab sitting up in an uncomfortable chair in the ICU waiting room.

"No, I don't think so." She glanced over at Martha. "Are you with us, Martha?"

At first Mary thought she might protest. Then her sister shrugged. "Why not? The worst she can do is not answer the door, right?"

Which is exactly what happened. First they went to the Bettencourt home, where they found the curtains closed and no lights lit. There was no window on the garage to confirm whether a car was inside, but the home had that no-one-is-here look.

A short drive away was Bettencourt Lumber Supply. The business was housed in a warehouse-like structure fronted by what appeared to be a log cabin that had been attached. Mary stepped out of the car and walked over to pull on the door handle.

"It's locked," she told her sisters when she returned to the car. "And I didn't see anyone inside the office."

"Probably because it's half past seven on a Sunday night," Elizabeth said patiently. "I'm going to drive around back and see what's going on there."

She eased her car into the narrow alley that ran behind the warehouse. Gravel crunched under their tires as they slowly rolled along until the back doors of the warehouse came into view. Elizabeth put the car into PARK.

"See anything?" she asked her sisters.

"Not a thing," Mary said as her eyes scanned the empty parking lot.

"Me neither," Martha said. "Though it looks like someone might have been here recently. There's a paper pinned to the loading dock doors. See it?"

Mary craned her neck to get a look at what her sister was describing. "I see something up there. It's yellow." She let out a long breath. "Oh for goodness' sake. Elizabeth, just drive up there, and I'll climb out and read it."

Elizabeth did as Mary said, slowing to a stop just beside the stairs that ran alongside the loading dock. Mary opened the door slowly, looking around before she made the climb up to the wide metal doors.

The sign fluttered in the breeze, making reading the thing nearly impossible. It looked like an advertising flyer for some fast food chain, but there was something scribbled on the back. It was as if the writer of the note left it on the first piece of paper he or she found, turning the ad around so the blank surface could be used for writing.

Writing with horrible penmanship.

Mary stepped back and pulled her phone out of her pocket and opened the camera. Then she held the paper down with one hand and took a photo of it with the other.

While she was standing there, she took the opportunity to look around to see what else was behind the lumber supply building. Other than several trash cans and a pile of wooden pallets stacked haphazardly next to a closed dumpster, there was nothing of note around.

Across the alley was a pasture. To the right was a small convenience store that looked as if it hadn't been open for business for a decade or more, and to the left was a forlorn-looking one-story office building with signs plastered on the windows that proclaimed it was "reduced" and "for lease or purchase."

Other than an empty Bettencourt Lumber delivery van parked at the back of the lot, there was nothing to indicate that humans might have traveled anywhere near this place recently. Mary went down the steps and returned to the car.

"Well?" Elizabeth asked. "What did the sign say?"

"I'm still trying to decipher it." Mary showed her sisters the picture she'd taken. "Any ideas?"

"Let me see that," Martha said. "I may be able to figure it out."

Mary handed her the phone and watched while her sister squinted to try to make out what was written there. Finally she shook her head.

"The screen is too small. Let's go home and bring it up on the computer. I bet it'll be readable then."

As it turned out, it was very readable despite the horrible penmanship. PLANS CHANGED. COME BACK AT 9.

Mary looked at the clock on the corner of the computer screen. "It's not even half past eight. I say we go back out there and see what's going on."

Elizabeth shrugged. "Why not?"

"Because it could be a drug deal or something," Martha said. "I vote we call the police and let them handle it."

"Call the police and tell them what?" Mary demanded. "That we were trespassing on Bettencourt Lumber property and found a note saying there's some kind of meeting at nine o'clock?" She lifted a shoulder. "Sure. Go ahead," she told her sister. "But I'm going with Elizabeth to see if we can find out just who that someone is."

Mary exchanged grins with Elizabeth, who rose, grabbed her purse and keys, and said, "If we're going to do this, we need to go now so we can figure out a place to hide the car and then watch to see who shows up."

"Oh, a stakeout." Mary stood up and turned to Martha, who was still seated at the desk. "Are you sure you won't come with us? You're going to miss all the fun."

Martha groaned. "Oh all right, but at the first sign of trouble, I'm calling the police."

A short while later, Elizabeth drove down the alley again and parked in the same spot where they'd been earlier. At fifteen minutes before nine, twilight was upon them, and the road was dark.

"Now what?" Elizabeth asked. "Where's the best place to wait?"

"How about if we park over there in the lot behind the convenience store?" Martha suggested. "It's far enough away and yet close enough to be able to see whatever happens at the loading dock."

The security light over the loading dock door cast a blue shadow around the dock but stopped short of illuminating the parking lot. Everything else was cast in shadows, but should a vehicle drive through, it would be seen immediately.

"I think that's too out in the open," Mary said. She paused to glance around. "I think we need to stash the car on the other side of the office building and come back over here. There are lots of places to hide."

"You mean get out of the car?" Martha's tone and expression left little to the imagination. She was not pleased with the suggestion.

"Yes," Mary said. "If we're going to avoid being seen, we have to do it that way. Do you want to risk missing out on whatever's going to happen at nine just because we were afraid?"

Martha looked like she just might say yes, she would take that risk if it meant not leaving the car. Elizabeth, however, shook her head. "No, I agree. It's too big of a chance to take. We have to try."

Under protest, Martha followed along as the three of them ditched the car on the other side of the abandoned office building and made the hike to the loading dock parking lot with five minutes to spare.

"Our best option is to hide behind the dumpster and pile of crates," Mary suggested when they paused behind a row of shrubs at the edge of the office building. "It's in the shadows but close enough to the loading dock to see what's going on."

"I don't know," Martha said. "It's awfully close to the dock. Maybe we should just stay right here. We can see everything, and it's less distance to the car if we have to make a run for it."

"True," Mary said, "but we can't see faces as well from this distance, and we certainly can't confront them."

"Why would we want to do that?" Elizabeth demanded. "We're here to observe. If we're going to answer this question of who's setting fire to Amish businesses, we need to be careful. The person we're looking for is dangerous."

"I agree," Mary said, "but if we're too careful, we'll miss the opportunity to—" A light glinted in the distance. "Well, maybe our decision has been made for us. I think I see a car coming this way."

Mary crouched down behind the shrubs, and her sisters joined her. Elizabeth immediately began to grumble about ruining her best skirt while Martha shifted positions and fussed about her arthritis in her knee.

"Next time, Elizabeth, change clothes before we go on a stakeout," Mary said. "And for goodness' sake, Martha, a little pain is worth what we could gain here tonight."

"If this wasn't coming from the youngest in the group, I might take it better," Martha snapped. "Your time is coming, Mary Classen Baxter. Just wait. You'll have joints popping and knees complaining just like we do."

"Shhh," Mary said as she nodded to the alley. "And tell your joints to be quiet too."

Martha gave her a playful nudge, and they shared a grin. "I repeat. Your day is coming, Mary Baxter."

As the lights drew near, the speed of their approach slowed. Finally the vehicle reached the edge of the parking lot and stopped. Though the light had faded to near complete darkness, and shadows lengthened, it was easy to tell this was a truck, not a car.

A blue light went on inside the cab of the truck. "Is the driver using his phone?" Elizabeth whispered.

"I think so," Martha said. "Maybe letting whoever he's meeting know he's here."

The blue light went off, and the truck lurched forward to swerve into the parking lot. After making a wide sweep, its headlights illuminating every inch of the perimeter of the lot—including the spot where they might have been had they elected to hide behind the dumpster and wooden pallets—it came to a stop beside the empty van.

There was something in the back of the truck, but it was impossible to see exactly what that might be in the dark. Definitely not a camper, but something large all the same. Whatever it was might not be visible now, but it would make the truck easy to identify in the daylight.

Headlights went out, dousing the truck in darkness once again. Only the circle of light from the lamp over the loading dock offered any visibility.

"Showtime," Mary whispered. "Now let's see who's in that truck."

CHAPTER ELEVEN

For what seemed like forever, nothing happened. The truck sat in darkness. Night birds chirped. Then Elizabeth made a squealing sound and jumped back.

Mary turned to make a face at her. "Shhh!"

"A bug was crawling on my arm," she protested.

"There are bugs?" Martha asked. "I did not sign up for bugs."

"Look," Mary said, "if either of you wants to go back to the car and wait for me there, please do. But if you're going to stay here and watch what happens in the parking lot, you're going to have to be quiet."

"Okay," Elizabeth said, though there was the slightest note of sarcasm in her tone. Martha elected not to respond. She was probably weighing her options, though Mary doubted her middle sister would want to return to the car and wait there alone.

The blue light went back on in the truck, illuminating a person as he hunched over what had to be his phone. Then the light went out again.

"This is just like in the movies," Elizabeth said.

"I hope it's not like one of those movies where the bad guy ends up shooting everyone." Martha shuddered. "I hate those movies."

"And I don't want to be shot," Elizabeth added.

A slapping sound indicated someone attempting to kill another bug. "Nor do I want to be eaten alive by mosquitoes, but here we are," Martha said.

"This isn't the first time we've followed a possible suspect," Mary told them. "Why are you two acting like this?"

"It is most definitely the first time I've found myself sitting in a bush after dark on an August night. It's hot, and there are mosquitoes. That's a new one for me. How about you, Elizabeth?"

"I certainly don't remember if I've done this before. I don't think so. And though you're right about the mosquitoes, they're not biting me. I think it might be your perfume. Mosquitoes love that."

"Mosquitoes love perfume?" Martha chuckled. "Well I wasn't going for attracting them, but that's good to know."

Mary fixed them with a please-be-quiet look, but her sisters weren't paying any attention. Not that either of them could see her very well in the gathering darkness.

She turned back around just in time to see the driver's door open on the delivery van. Then, as if in slow motion, a dark figure slid out of the van and crouched down beside it. Mary nudged Martha. "The van wasn't empty," she whispered. "It's a person dressed in black."

"Just like the movies," her sisters said in unison.

The dark figure scurried to the truck and opened the passenger door. The dome light came on, briefly showing a person in a black hoodie climbing inside. Mary turned her attention to the driver. Before she could identify anything other than a denim jacket and a baseball cap, the light went off again.

Abruptly the truck's lights blazed.

"They're leaving," Mary said. "We have to follow them."

"Wait," Martha said as Mary and Elizabeth started back to the car. "Let's see which way they turn out of the parking lot, and then we'll know which way to go."

They watched as the truck turned right onto the street, and then they ran to the car. They threw the doors open and hurled themselves onto the seats. Elizabeth started the engine and buckled her seat belt at the same time and then headed for the exit.

"Don't act like you're in a hurry," Mary told Elizabeth as they saw the truck's rear lights ahead. "There isn't much traffic, so we should be able to keep them in sight without getting too close."

Elizabeth did as she was told then glanced over at Mary. "I think we need to let the police know what we're doing. That truck could be going anywhere, and who knows who that person in black is?"

"Elizabeth is right," Martha said. "This could have nothing to do with the arson case. There could be a drug deal going down or worse. We certainly don't want to be caught in the middle of it."

Mary frowned. "What are we going to tell them? We waited in a parking lot until a truck picked up a guy in a hoodie, and now we're following them?" She thought a moment. "No, I think this has everything to do with the arsonist. I'm just not sure exactly how it's connected. But I heard what I heard, and I know that Julie knows something about the fires."

"I agree," Elizabeth said. "When she spoke to John about a private citizen's obligation to tell what she knows, I felt like she knew something important that she would eventually be telling law enforcement. Something important enough to call off coffee with her friend and hurry away even though the friend was sitting right there."

"That's why I think she knows something rather than she did something," Martha said. "If she did something, the last person she would talk to about it is a police officer, especially in front of someone she knows."

"It does make sense," Mary said. "But why was she so angry? I'm telling you, I was stunned at how mad she looked. Though Caleb was able to calm her down, or at least that's how it looked to me before I walked away from the window. Jake may tell a different story. He stood there longer than I did."

"Okay," Elizabeth said, "I see your point in not calling the police, but does anyone have an objection to calling John? I just don't want us out here following someone without anyone knowing what we're doing. It doesn't seem safe."

"Yes, that's a good idea," Martha said.

Mary added her nod. Elizabeth handed Mary her phone, and a few minutes later, John's voice came through the car's speakers.

"I have you on the car phone," Elizabeth told him. "I'm driving. Mary and Martha are with me."

John greeted them then said, "I get the impression something is going on. Do I want to know what it is?"

"Well," Elizabeth said slowly, "it seems I'm following a truck right now."

A low chuckle rumbled through the speakers, and then he said, "That seems pretty harmless."

"Normally it would be, but—"

"Look, they're turning onto the highway," Martha cried. "Don't lose them. See, they're just ahead of that eighteen-wheeler."

"Elizabeth," John said slowly, "what are you doing? Specifically and not generally. I know you're following a truck. For what purpose?"

"I'm going to let Mary tell you. Martha is busy watching, and I'm just trying not to get caught following them."

"Okay," Mary said, "Elizabeth needs to concentrate on driving. So the short version is we went looking for Julie and found what might be her escape. Or a drug deal. Or something shady involving a pickup and a van and a person in a black hoodie. So we're following them. They're in a pickup."

There was a moment of silence. "Yeah, um, I'm going to need the long version, Mary."

So she told him everything, then she paused. "So now we're following them to see where they're going. I can't think of a reason why someone would be hiding in the Bettencourt Lumber delivery van and then getting picked up by a mysterious truck following a note left on a loading dock door, but that's what's happening."

He sighed. "Okay, did you get a plate number?"

"No, we weren't close enough," Elizabeth said. "But it's a white pickup truck with something big in the back."

"Not a camper," Martha said.

"Definitely not a camper," Elizabeth agreed.

"Any idea where they're heading?" John asked.

"No clue," Elizabeth told him. "I'm staying back and keeping a few cars between us, but so far they're just driving west on the freeway."

"West, okay. Let me see if I have any buddies in the area who can get eyes on the vehicle. Hang on just a minute. I'm going to have to put you on hold." He came back after a few minutes. "Okay, so no description of the driver and passenger that I can pass along?"

"The driver had on a baseball cap and a denim jacket. The passenger was wearing all black with a hoodie over his head. I couldn't see anything else." Mary turned to her sisters. "Do either of you have anything to add to that?"

Both women shook their heads. "I can say that the passenger wasn't tall. And he was thin," Elizabeth said. "Other than that, we saw the same thing Mary did."

"Okay, I've got a guy out by the airport. I'm going to have him swing around and meet you, but I'll need your coordinates so he can meet up with you."

Mary nodded to the vehicle they were following. "No need, John. It looks like our truck is heading right toward him. They're signaling to take the airport exit."

"Okay, hang on." And he was gone again.

Mary spied the lights atop the airport's control tower up ahead. Then she saw the flash of red and blue lights off in the distance.

The truck was already on the exit ramp slowing down, and Elizabeth was now almost behind them. Just one vehicle separated her from the truck. Unfortunately it was a massive delivery van just large enough to block their view.

"Do you still see the truck?" John asked.

"I can't see it, but I know it's in front of the van in front of me," Elizabeth told him. "We're all stuck at a red light. I also see police lights. Is that your friend?"

He muttered something and said, "Hold on." After a second, the lights disappeared. Then John returned. "I told him not to run hot. It'll spook the driver. He should have turned off his lights by now. Do you still see them?"

"No," Elizabeth said, and Mary and Martha concurred.

"Okay, he's coming in from the opposite direction, so he's going to try and turn around to see if he can grab a plate number. Depending on what he finds, he'll pull them over. You ladies just stay safe and wait for him."

The light turned green, but the truck had not yet moved. "Look out, he's turning left!" Martha called from the back seat.

"Left?" John asked. "Is there a left turn there?"

"Not exactly," Elizabeth said. "There's a dirt road that goes who knows where."

Which was exactly where the truck was going. Maybe the driver had seen the flashing lights and wanted no part of an encounter with a police cruiser.

But the cruiser was too fast for them. The lights and siren came back on, and the police car followed the truck onto the dirt road. The truck immediately pulled to the side of the road and stopped.

Traffic was piling up behind her, so Elizabeth turned left onto the dirt road also and parked immediately on the side, putting her car about twenty yards behind the two other vehicles.

"John," she said, "are you still there? I've got a plate number for you."

She read out the number to him. "I think it's some sort of wrecker. It's dark, and the lights aren't doing a great job of illuminating it, but I think the thing in the back looks like a hook."

"That's because it is," John said. "You've been following a truck registered to Chester's Autos."

"Oh no, they stole a truck too?" Martha exclaimed.

"Stay back, Elizabeth," John said. "I'm listening to the takedown now on the scanner. The perps are still in the stolen truck, so be careful. One or both of them could have a gun, so you need to turn around and go home. Someone can come and get your statements there."

"Another day, another statement," Mary said on an exhale of breath as she watched the doors of the police cruiser fly open and two officers jump out with guns drawn.

"Just like the movies," Martha said.

The officers, one man and one woman, inched toward the stolen truck until the male officer shouted, "Driver, come out with your hands up."

Nothing happened.

The officer repeated the demand, and this time the door opened. A moment later, the driver stepped out into the circle of lights made by the police car's headlights.

"Oh my goodness!" Elizabeth said. "It can't be!"

CHAPTER TWELVE

H enri Sessions?" Mary frowned. "Surely not."
But it was. This became plain when the officer motioned
for her to take off her cap.

Oh no. Something had gone terribly wrong. Mary opened
the car door and climbed out.

She heard Elizabeth's voice behind her. "Mary! Come back
here. John said we need to leave."

But Mary just kept walking. She had to help Henri.
"Officers, this isn't a car thief," she called as she walked toward
them. "I know this woman."

Mary froze at the same time the male police officer
demanded she do so. There was a passenger in the truck, a
passenger dressed in black who had slipped out of the dark van
earlier and had not, as of yet, stepped out of the tow truck.

"Henri, if you were forced to do all this against your will,
tell the officers now. I'll back you up," Mary called.

Henri looked over to meet her gaze. "No, this one's on me.
It was my choice."

"You chose to steal the tow truck?" Mary asked as the male
police officer frowned at her. "Why would you do that?"

"Ma'am," the officer told her, "I know you're a friend of
John Marks, but you're going to have to step back. This scene is
not yet secure, and I can't have you speaking with the suspect."

Mary held out her hands. "But Officer, Henri isn't a suspect. She works at the auto shop."

He gave her a look that told her he didn't care where Henri worked. "Step. Back."

Mary took two steps backward. She glanced behind her to see that Elizabeth and Martha had made no move to join her.

Slowly the female officer was moving toward the closed passenger door. Meanwhile, the other officer placed Henri in handcuffs.

"Okay, passenger," the female officer called as she wrenched open the passenger door. "Keep your hands where I can see them and exit the vehicle slowly. Step out with your back to me, hands in the air."

The figure in black emerged like a ghoul from the depths of the tow truck then paused to wait for instructions. Mary watched in fascination. It truly was just like in the movies.

"All right, passenger, now start taking steps backward in my direction. Follow the sound of my voice until I tell you to stop."

The passenger stood very still and did not respond.

"Better do what they say," Henri called. "We'll only get in a whole lot worse trouble if you don't."

Then, to Mary's astonishment, she heard a female voice answer Henri.

"I can't walk backward. I'll fall. Just let me turn around. I don't have anything on me that can hurt anyone except maybe the nail file in my bag."

That voice. It was familiar.

Elizabeth stepped out of the car and hurried to join Mary. "Mary, do you know who that is?"

"Who?" she asked her sister before returning her attention to the scene unfolding before her.

"It's Julie Bettencourt."

Julie held her head high as the female officer hurried to place her in handcuffs and walk her to the patrol car. Though her eyes met Mary's, she said nothing.

"Okay, lady," the officer told Julie as she helped her fold into the police car without hitting her head, "is there anything you want to say for yourself?"

Silence.

"Bring the driver over," she told her partner. "This one isn't talking."

"I want my lawyer," Julie said.

When the prisoners were secured in the back seat of the police car, the female officer climbed into the passenger seat.

"Are they being arrested?" Elizabeth asked the other officer as he went around the cruiser to the driver's side.

"That remains to be seen. Marks briefed us on what you saw, but until we get some kind of statement from these two or can confirm whether the truck was stolen or used with the employer's permission, there may not be much to hold them on." He opened the driver's door. "We'll take these two to the station and see if we can't figure out what they're up to. The truck will be impounded, and if they stole it, we'll search it."

"If it helps," Mary said, "it looked as if they were headed for the airport until they saw the flashing lights. That's when they turned off onto the dirt road."

"We may need statements from you three if it turns out anything illegal was going on in that parking lot. I'll let my boss sort that out." He climbed in the car and started the engine. A moment later they pulled away.

Mary followed Elizabeth back to the car. As they turned around to head toward the main road, she tried to make sense of what she'd seen.

Finally, she said what she was thinking. "Okay, what just happened here? Henri picked up Julie, who was hiding in a van outside her loading dock. They were likely heading to the airport, and my guess would be that meant they were fleeing. Julie was dressed in black, and Henri was wearing a baseball cap." She shook her head. "Does that mean we put Julie back in as a suspect and add Henri as an accomplice?"

Silence.

Mary tried again. "Am I the only one thinking this?"

"No, you said everything I'm thinking too," Martha said as Elizabeth nodded. "I just can't make it all add up."

"Nor can I," Elizabeth said.

"Crimes don't always make sense," John said, causing them all to scream.

"John!" Elizabeth snapped. "I didn't know you were still on the phone."

"Of course I am," he said. "No way was I going to hang up with you three out in the middle of nowhere at an active crime scene. As to your question about Sessions and Bettencourt, sometimes it's the least likely person who turns out to be the one who did it."

"But Julie Bettencourt?" Elizabeth asked. "What in the world? Surely she wasn't setting those fires. But then, why was she heading for the airport? Or at least that's how it appears."

"She knows something," John said. "Remember what she said at the coffee shop?"

"So if she knows something," Mary said, "maybe she was trying to hide until she could get out of town in order to keep from...what? What would she be afraid of?"

"Retribution," Martha offered. "If the arsonist knows Julie knows something, then she would have reason to want to leave town."

"Not if she had police protection," Elizabeth protested. "Something doesn't add up. And why involve Henri?"

"Maybe Henri is the arsonist," Martha said. "Oh! And maybe Julie was blackmailing Henri."

"That sounds like a bad movie," John said. "More likely Julie somehow convinced Henri she needed to get out of town quick and without being seen. She was willing to pay to make that happen."

Mary blew out a long breath. "But why would she involve Henri?"

Mary was still asking herself that question the next morning as she went about her duties at Secondhand Blessings. It was a busy morning, and all anyone could talk about was the fires. Though it was difficult not to join in and add her opinion to the others that were being given as the shoppers mingled about, she kept her silence on the matter.

The truth was, until all the facts were known, there was nothing that specifically pointed toward one person as the guilty party. And it was completely possible that the person they were looking for was someone Mary didn't even know.

Martha arrived a few minutes later, her arms full of baked goods to add to the first round of items she'd brought before the store opened. After last night's excitement, they'd all gone to bed, which meant that Martha had baking to catch up on this morning.

Thus she appeared a bit bleary-eyed but still smiling as she set the last loaf of cinnamon bread into place on the shelf and turned around to face Mary. Elizabeth came in from the office to admire her work.

"You've outdone yourself, Martha," she said. "I think the cinnamon bread is a great addition. As you can see, we sold out all the loaves we had this morning."

"About that." Martha looked around the empty store and then back at her sisters. "You both shared your news, but I didn't realize until this morning that I never shared mine."

"Oh," Mary said, instantly feeling terrible about slighting her sister. "I'm so sorry. We should have remembered that you had news too. What is it?"

Martha paused as if she was having trouble deciding on the words to use. Then she shrugged. "It seems as though I may be branching out."

"Branching out?" Mary asked. "How do you mean?"

"As in looking into a storefront." Martha looked over at Elizabeth. "Catherine Randall sent me an email. She said she'd spoken with you about a friend who was looking to sell her bakery to see if I was interested. Why didn't you tell me? Did you think I couldn't do it?"

Hurt flashed in Elizabeth's eyes. She said, "Oh, Martha, I'm sorry. I completely forgot. Yes, Catherine gave me her card when John and I were at Un-Common Grounds on Saturday afternoon. It's in my purse. I'll go up to the house and get it for you."

"No need," Martha said. "I already spoke to her friend. I'm meeting with her tomorrow afternoon."

"Oh?" Elizabeth said, her expression unreadable. "Well, how about that?" Her smile didn't reach all the way to her eyes.

"Elizabeth," Martha said gently. "You didn't answer my question. Not really. Okay, so you forgot. A lot has happened since Saturday afternoon." She paused. "But do you think I can run my own bakery?"

"Can you?" Elizabeth nodded. "Absolutely. You're a fabulous baker, and you have a great head for business. So of course you can."

"But?" Martha offered.

"But I just don't know if you should," Elizabeth admitted.

Martha looked over at Mary. "What's your opinion?"

"Mine?" She swallowed hard, hating to be put on the spot. "My opinion is, if it makes you happy, and it's what you want to do, then you should do it. And yes, I agree with Elizabeth. There's no doubt you can. As to whether you should? That's something you have to decide. We're your sisters, and we love you and want the best for you. But we don't get to decide what you do. That's up to you, Martha."

"Yes, okay," she said. "I've been praying about it, and I just don't know. On the one hand it's such a great possibility that it's almost a dream come true."

"It is?" Mary asked, surprised.

"No, that's not right," Martha said. "It's a dream I never dared to dream. But on the other hand..." She paused to look away. "Well, on the other hand, I don't know how it would work for me to be part of my own dream and part of the dream of Secondhand Blessings all at the same time."

"Nor do I," Elizabeth said.

Martha returned her attention to Elizabeth. "I don't think I could do both."

"And that's my concern," Elizabeth told her. "I'm being selfish, I know, but that's the first thing I thought of when Catherine told me about the opportunity."

"But," Mary offered, "any business where you bake the products you sell is going to be a stellar success."

Mary's phone buzzed, and she looked down to see who was calling. Jake hadn't updated her since she left the hospital yesterday, not that she expected him to.

But it wasn't Jake. It was the same number that had rung twice on Sunday.

CHAPTER THIRTEEN

Mary looked at her sisters and then sighed. "I'm sorry. I need to get this."

They nodded and returned to their conversation. Mary stepped into the back room and sat down on the nearest stool.

"Mary Baxter?" a male voice asked. "Do I have the right number?"

"Yes, this is Mary."

"Oh good," came out on an exhale of breath. "This is Augie. Augie Meyers? We met on Saturday when I bought some of your art to take to my gallery in Philadelphia."

"Augie, yes," she said as realization hit her. "Of course I remember."

"I was afraid I had the wrong number."

"Yes, sorry. I've had some things happen that kept me busy and prevented me from answering my phone." She paused only a beat. "How can I help you, Augie?"

"You can tell me whether you've got time to come to Philadelphia."

"I guess that would depend on when you want me to come," she said. "Why?"

"Remember how I told you I was considering putting some of your pieces in my gallery? Well, I had a show last night, and I sold a few pieces beforehand that were intended for the exhibit. Since that left room on the walls, I decided to toss in some of your work to see if there was any interest."

Her heart skipped a beat. "My work was in a gallery show in Philly last night?"

"*Was* being the operative word. I sold out of almost everything I put in the show. Apparently barns and buggies are hot right now. I thought as much, and that's why I took all of those you had. The other stuff didn't sell so well."

Barns and buggies? She'd painted a depiction of Rachel's buggy in their driveway, its stark black simplicity setting off the fire and brilliancy of the fall leaves above and all around it. She'd painted the same picture in several sizes, not sure which was the best. But "barns and buggies" certainly wasn't what she wanted to be known for. Was it?

"So I have a proposition," he continued. "You bring me more pieces, and I'll do a show with your works. Not exclusively yours," he cautioned. "But enough of yours to put your name in the catalog and get your work talked about. What do you say?"

"What do I say? I say I'm flattered, Augie. Surprised. And, well...speechless."

"So that's a yes?"

Mary laughed. "It sounds wonderful. I have some pieces I would love to have in a gallery. Some landscapes, wildlife, and nature scenes. I've been thinking about how I could get my work out there."

"Um, okay," Augie said. "Those sound nice, but what I want are the ones you paint with the Amish stuff. Like I said, barns, buggies, windmills, gardens, men plowing a field with a couple of big ol' draft horses. Amish kids, barefoot and dressed alike on their way to school." He paused. "I'm looking at putting the show together in a relatively short time. How many pieces can you send me if I were to set it for mid-October?"

Considering she had none like he described even started, Mary wasn't sure. "Well," she countered, "how many would you like?"

"Can you do twenty?"

She sputtered to a laugh. "Twenty? No, that's not possible." She took a deep breath. "Besides, Augie…why do you want just Amish pictures?"

"That's what's selling now," he said. "People can't get enough of it. The rest of your stuff is pretty good, sure, and shows talent, but what flew off the walls last night was that buggy one."

"I don't know, Augie," she said slowly. "I don't know if I want to box myself in like that."

"Well, that's certainly up to you," he said. "But you might change your mind when I tell you how much you can expect to make from each sale."

He quoted an amount that made her sure she'd heard wrong.

"Excuse me," she said. "Would you say that again?" He did. "Okay," Mary said on an exhale of breath, "I guess I should have upped my prices at the art fair on Saturday, then."

"I did feel a bit guilty that I paid so little. But I'm a businessman, and well, as I said, I had no idea Philadelphia would go for buggies and barns."

Buggies and barns. Was that how she wanted to be known in the art world? Huh. If the art world was paying what

Augie said they were paying, maybe she'd paint whatever they wanted.

"Okay, Mary," Augie said slowly. "You think about it and then tell me what's possible. Be realistic, but I want you to push yourself to get as many done as you possibly can. So with that in mind, send me that number by the end of the month, okay? If you're interested, that is. In the meantime, what's your email address? I want to send you the details."

"Sure, okay." Mary gave him her address then added, "Did you really sell all my Amish paintings? You're not just saying that."

"I did," he told her. "Well, the ones I put in the show. I kept the one I liked. The barns and buggies all sold."

There was that barns and buggies statement again. Why did it bother her so much?

They chatted for a few more minutes and then hung up. Mary walked back into the store to find that a few customers were now roaming the aisles, and Martha was busy helping another shopper at the register. The door opened to admit three more ladies who looked intent on buying.

Mary smiled. Their grandparents had opened this shop many years ago. Then Mama and Daddy ran it, until Daddy died and Mama got too sick. The shop closed for a few years, and it became the sisters' dream to have it up and running again. Now here it was, and doing a brisk business, especially since they'd been featured on a Christmas cooking show on the Dining and Décor Network last December.

The three of them made a great team. And they'd made their dream of reviving Secondhand Blessings come true.

And yet Martha was poised to possibly leave and start her own bakery. Mary was considering a career painting barns and buggies for big bucks. Where did that leave Secondhand Blessings?

Mary shook off the question and tucked her phone away, then went back out into the store. She spied Rachel Fischer and her youngest child and smiled.

"I didn't realize you were working today," she said to Rachel.

"I just came to speak with you." She looked at Dorcas. "Please give me a moment with Mrs. Baxter." Once the littlest Fischer had settled in to play in the children's area, Rachel continued. "I came to ask if there is truth to the rumor that the federal government is coming to investigate the fires."

"I've heard the same thing, Rachel. Yes, it could happen."

Rachel looked concerned. "Why?"

"The last fire was set in a building while church services were going on. That elevates the crime to a federal crime. At least that's how it was explained to me."

Rachel nodded. "Yes, the Hershberger fire. He remained in the building until he was certain everyone else was safe. It was a brave thing to do." She paused. "Others fought the fire and were burned. Also brave. Had they not, there would have been more injuries and possibly deaths."

Mary shook her head. "This person needs to be stopped, Rachel. I feel so helpless, and yet my sisters and I are determined to do what we can to find out who is setting these fires."

"And that is why I am here," she said. "I hoped that you would tell me you and your sisters are investigating. Any help you need that I can provide is freely offered."

"Thank you," Mary said. "I very much appreciate that. Could you make it known that we are also looking for this person?"

Rachel smiled. "I will do what I can. The Lord does not give us a spirit of fear, but I will rest easier when this person is caught."

Later that afternoon when things were quiet at the store, Mary went to the office and sent Jake a text asking about Caleb. His answer came a few moments later.

ENCOURAGED WITH HIS PROGRESS AND CAUTIOUSLY OPTI-MISTIC WITH HIS PROGNOSIS. ANY NEWS ON THE SEARCH FOR WHO DID THIS?

Mary thought a moment and then typed a brief reply.

JULIE BETTENCOURT AND HENRI SESSIONS ARE IN CUSTODY BUT NOT UNDER ARREST. LONG STORY.

Martha came in just as Mary sent the text. "I think we need to interview the business owners who have been targeted. I'm going to use my lunchtime to speak to Amos Mast. If the store isn't busy when I'm done, I'll go over to the hardware store in New Holland. Do you want to come with me?"

"Sure," Mary tucked her phone into her pocket. "As long as Elizabeth doesn't mind watching the store alone."

"She doesn't," Martha said. "I already asked."

A few minutes later, they pulled up in front of Masts' Furniture. Martha had called ahead, so Amos was waiting for them in his office when they stepped inside.

"Yes, I argued with Caleb," he said after they'd been seated and the greetings dispensed with. "I spoke with Rachel Fischer," he told them. "So if you had not paid me a visit, I would have come to you."

"Do you have any idea who set that fire?" Martha asked.

He shook his head. "I do not."

"Do you think it was Caleb?" Mary watched his face carefully.

"No." He paused. "Caleb and I argued about a furniture design. He says it is his original work, and I say it is mine. That is no reason to destroy a man's business."

"Are you speaking about his business or yours?" Mary asked.

His eyes narrowed. "Both," he finally said.

"So a fight over a design, and then you were friends again?" Martha shrugged. "No hard feelings? Just like that?"

"Until I made a mistake and said something I regret." He paused. "His wife, Anna. I should never have questioned whether she was a proper wife for him. It was said in anger. I went out to the farm to apologize to him, but he was not there. I conveyed my apologies to his wife. Before I could speak to him personally, the fire occurred."

"So you went out to see Caleb," Mary said, "but you spoke with Anna alone. When was that?"

"I would never speak to his wife alone," he said. "Her sister was with her. That was the day before the fire here."

"If you don't think Caleb did this," Martha said gently, "then do you have an idea who might have?"

He looked away before returning his attention to Martha. It appeared as if he might have someone in mind. Then he shook his head. "I have no idea."

"What about Julie Bettencourt or Henri Sessions?" Martha asked. "Could one of them be the guilty party?"

"Why would either of them want to burn the businesses of the Amish? Mrs. Bettencourt does business with us. I do not know this Sessions person, so perhaps. But again, what would be the reason? I heard that she works in an auto repair shop, ja?"

"She does," Martha told him. "There was also a fire at the Amish-owned hardware store in New Holland that started in a manner similar to the one here. Were you aware of that?"

"Our community is acutely aware of all of the fires," he said. "And we are concerned."

"Why do you think this is happening?" Mary asked.

He seemed to give the question a moment's thought. "These fires seem to be planned, not spontaneous, and I do not believe the arsonist is choosing victims at random. The problem is finding the link between them all."

"What is the link, Amos?" Martha asked. "Do you have any idea?"

Amos paused. "My guess is someone with poor control over his temper is taking offense and turning it into revenge."

Mary studied him for a moment. Though he seemed to be forthcoming with his answers, she got the distinct impression he was not telling her everything. "Who other than Caleb has taken offense with you lately?"

His brows rose. She thought he might give her a name, maybe two. Then he shrugged. "No one."

"Could the arsonist be Amish?" Martha asked.

A moment passed, and Amos did not speak. "The arsonist could be anyone," he finally said. "I cannot be more helpful than that."

Could not or would not? Mary wasn't sure.

"What do you know about the print and sign store in Lancaster that was targeted?"

"Mr. Hershberger is the owner. There was a church meeting going on in the back, and apparently he was very heroic in making sure everyone got out safe. He was injured." Amos paused. "I have wondered since I heard about this one whether the person who set the fire knew that meeting was in progress or not."

Mary considered that. She let out a long breath. If the person behind these attacks knew there was a meeting going on when they set the fire, then they were indeed escalating the level of violence. There was no guessing what would come next.

"Thank you," Mary said as she stood. "You've raised some good questions."

"And given you some answers you were seeking, I hope."

Martha smiled and rose to her feet. "I think perhaps you have."

"If we have more questions, may we come back and ask them?" Mary asked.

"You may," he said slowly. "But I will likely be of no help."

Mary followed her sister out of the back office and across the showroom floor of Masts' Furniture. The pieces on display here were lovely. It was easy to see how Caleb might want to compare his work to what the store had to offer.

Or, Mary thought, Amos Mast also might compare what he had here to what Caleb could make.

Mary held her thoughts until she reached the car. "He's hiding something," she finally said as Martha pulled out of the parking lot. "I don't know what it is, but there's something he isn't telling us. Probably something the Amish know that they don't want the Englisch to know."

"That doesn't sound very nice," Martha said. "And you're speculating. You don't know that for a fact."

She thought a moment. "I don't mean it to be unkind. But didn't you feel it too?"

"Maybe," Martha said. "Or it could just be that Amos wasn't comfortable speaking with women, or with us in his office, or any number of other reasons."

"I suppose." Before Mary could say anything else, her phone rang. She glanced down. "It's Jake."

"Mary," he said when she answered. "Caleb is awake, and he's asking for you."

"I'll be right there." She hung up and then glanced over at her sister. "I know we were heading for New Holland, but would you mind terribly if that waited for later? Caleb wants to talk to me."

"I don't mind." Martha shrugged. "I can run my errand after I drop you off at the hospital."

"You sure?"

"Absolutely." She smiled. "It's a good sign that Caleb is awake and wanting to talk, isn't it?"

"I hope so," Mary said. "I've been giving Jake his space, but I've wanted to go up and visit more than once. It's frustrating not knowing how Caleb is doing other than the brief texts I get from Jake."

"You like him a lot, don't you?" Martha asked.

"Jake?" Mary furrowed her brows. "He's an old friend, so sure. I like him." At Martha's grin, she frowned. "What? Are you thinking I'm interested in him?"

Her sister shrugged. "I wouldn't blame you. He's handsome. He's a doctor, for goodness' sake, and he's very nice. He seems to like you as well."

"Martha, you have got to be kidding," Mary exclaimed, unable to believe that her sister imagined some romantic relationship could develop between her and Jake Miller in the very short time since he'd returned to Bird-in-Hand.

"No?" was her cryptic response. "Well, okay then."

"Martha," Mary said slowly, "has Jake said something to you? Because I don't want him to misunderstand our friendship."

"No, nothing at all," she said. "And maybe I misunderstood. I mean, you and Jake have been through a lot together since he returned."

"Yes we have." She paused. "I'm just glad Caleb is better. I can't imagine what it would be like to lose one of you. And Caleb is his only brother."

"I wonder if his sisters will be coming in to see him," Martha said. "If I remember right, they both live in Florida now."

They rode the rest of the way to the hospital in companionable silence. Just before Martha pulled into the parking lot, Mary reached over to touch her sleeve. "You surprised me with your news."

"I could tell." She pulled into a parking space near the main doors and put the car into PARK. "I'm still wondering why Elizabeth didn't tell me."

"A lot happened on Saturday," Mary offered. "Don't read anything into that. I'm sure she would have given you the information if it had been any other day."

Martha offered a weak smile. "But it definitely wasn't any other day, was it?"

"It was not." Mary sighed and rested her head on her headrest. "I'm a little worried about going in to see Caleb. I don't want to upset him by getting upset. Okay, that sounds silly, but you know what I mean, right? He's been in a fire, Martha."

"He's asking for you," she said gently. "You'll do fine. Let's pray about it, okay?"

Martha grasped Mary's hand and bowed her head. "Lord, You are the great healer. If it is Your will, please heal Caleb. And make Mary's visit a good one. Give her the words to say to provide comfort to Caleb. I pray for Jake too. For his strength, and for peace. Amen."

"Amen." Mary opened her eyes and smiled then reached for the door handle. "Thank you." She paused. "Are you coming in?"

"No, I don't think it would be a good idea. Caleb asked for you, so you need to be the only one who goes in." She was silent a moment. "I've got errands I can run. Just call me when you're ready for me to come get you."

"Okay then." Mary stepped out into the afternoon sun and closed the door behind her. Though the walk to the door was brief, she arrived at the hospital's main doors far too quickly. The elevator reached the ICU floor even faster.

Somehow a moment later, she was standing at the door.

Then the code blue signal blared.

CHAPTER FOURTEEN

artha's GPS indicated that her destination was ahead one block on the right. She pulled into a parking space then climbed out of the car and tucked her keys into her pocket.

From where she stood, she could see the turquoise and white striped awning fluttering in the afternoon breeze. As she moved closer, the tatters at the edges were visible.

Nothing that couldn't be repaired.

She picked up her pace, pausing only to stop at the corner and allow a car to pass. Then she crossed the road and arrived on the block where the Sweet Shop was located.

The stores on either side of it were of the quaint variety— one sold candles, and the other specialized in handwoven linens and bedding—and there was an apartment upstairs that might or might not come with the building.

She stuttered to a stop as the fire-engine-red door opened, and a woman stepped out with three fair-haired little girls in tow. Each had some sort of treat in her hand. Martha's heart twinged as she thought of her own children. Of her grandchildren.

How they would love visits to their grandmother's shop!

Two lemon-yellow benches sat out front, one centered in front of each of the windows that looked into the interior of the shop. Pots of red geraniums provided a pop of color on each end of the benches.

Martha bypassed the door and sat on a bench. Swiveling, she looked inside, where a steady stream of customers enjoyed treats at tables that followed the same color theme as the exterior.

She made mental notes of what she liked, what she would change, and what was included in the price of the shop. Then she retrieved a notebook from her bag and wrote them all down.

Sitting back on the bench, she looked at her list. It wasn't long. But it wasn't short.

This shop would take some work. And a massive loan from the bank.

But she was starting to consider the option. It wasn't exactly a dream come true yet, because she hadn't allowed herself to dream this. It could be though.

Maybe.

An Amish woman stepped outside with a tray holding two cups of coffee and two paper-wrapped treats. Rather than walk away, she smiled down at Martha.

"May I join you?"

"Oh, yes, of course." Martha moved over and made room for the tiny woman with the big blue eyes and broad smile.

"I brought this for you." She nodded to the coffee and treats then grinned. "I only added a little sugar to the coffee. If you eat that cookie over it, that will add the rest of the flavor."

"Thank you." Martha accepted the coffee and cookie and then shook her head. "What a nice thing to do."

"Not really," she said. "I recognized you from Secondhand Blessings. My nephew is one of your suppliers." She met Martha's gaze. "And I am the owner of this shop that you're interested in buying."

Martha wasn't sure what to say. "I don't yet know if I'm interested. I guess you could say I'm exploring the option."

A dip of the Amish woman's head acknowledged the statement. "Well, in any case, I am Eunice Rohrer. And you are Martha Classen Watts."

"Yes." Martha smiled. "I'm pleased to meet you, Mrs. Rohrer."

"And I you, although since I was acquainted with your parents I feel as though I know you as well. If you do not mind, I will leave the business talk to those who are best at it. My son is the man you will need to speak to about the price of this store and what comes with the purchase." She paused. "I am a baker, a mother, and a wife, Mrs. Watts. It just turns out I have also become a businesswoman in my old age."

"I understand," Martha said. "I find myself in a similar position. I do wonder if the apartment above comes with the purchase."

"It does," she said. "Do you have grandchildren?"

The change of topic jarred Martha, but she quickly warmed to it. Any time she was given the opportunity to talk about the little loves of her life, she took it. "I have five. Four grandsons and one granddaughter."

Mrs. Rohrer's smile was immediate. "What a lovely gift from God. I have fourteen as of now with another three expected. Saul and I are blessed. Busy," she said with a chuckle, "but blessed."

"Fourteen going on seventeen. Yes you are," Martha exclaimed. "Both busy and blessed."

The Amish woman's smile faded. "Caleb Miller was meant to die in that explosion."

"Excuse me." A nurse brushed past Mary to press the button on the wall that opened the doors to the Intensive Care Unit.

Mary stepped back, the clanging of the code blue alarm echoing in her ears. "Can you tell me which room the alarm is for?" she called to the nurse's departing back.

"ICU Four," she said over her shoulder as she hurried away.

Mary let out a long breath. Caleb was in ICU Three.

The door slammed inches from her face. A moment later, the code blue alarm ceased.

Mary stood there unable to move. Then she turned around and nearly crashed into Abigail Byler.

Abigail was the opposite of her sister in just about every way. Where Anna was tiny and frail with thin dark hair and angry brown eyes, Abigail was robust and the picture of health with bright auburn curls that were barely tamed by her black kapp. The only sign she was a bit older than her sister were the fine lines at the corners of her eyes. Mary's last memory of Anna's eyes were of brown daggers of fury, and looking at Mary now were two blue eyes full of concern.

"Oh." Mary gasped. "Abigail. You're here. We've been wondering where you've been. Are you all right?"

Abigail touched Mary's arm. "Was that code blue for Caleb?" she finally asked, ignoring Mary's concern for her.

"No," Mary told her. "It wasn't."

Relief washed over her features. "So Caleb is not dead."

A statement, not a question. Thus, Mary felt no need to respond. Instead, she nodded to the waiting room. "Why don't you come and sit with me?"

Abigail paused, seemingly reluctant to follow Mary. Then she turned that way. "Yes, all right."

They were the only ones in the waiting room. Mary took a chair in the corner opposite the coffee cart and then waited for Abigail to join her.

"Where have you been?" Mary finally asked her.

"Away," she said, not meeting Mary's gaze. "Anna and I had a disagreement not long after you and Caleb's brother left the farm on Saturday. I could not stay."

Mary studied the Amish woman. With her black kapp indicating her status as a single woman and her typically modest clothing, nothing marked her as different from others of her faith.

"There have been several fires in the area," Mary said. "Did you know that?"

She returned her attention to Mary, and there was a sadness in her eyes. "Yes."

"Where did you go?"

"Away," she repeated. She toyed with the hem of her sleeve, her nails frayed as if she'd been biting them. "To a place where Anna could not find me."

Mary was startled. "Did you think you were in danger, Abigail?"

A moment passed, and then Abigail started crying. She took a handkerchief out of the pocket of her dress and wiped her eyes. "I know Anna and what she can do when she gets angry. My parents hoped that my presence would help her cope, but they did not consider that things might spin out of my control."

Mary's mouth dropped open. "So you are afraid of her?"

No response. Then Abigail said, "Mary, I love my sister. I would do anything in the world for her. But I'm afraid for her." She wiped more tears from her eyes.

There was a long pause as a pair of nurses walked by in the hall, chattering about a patient. Then silence fell between them again.

"She's being held for questioning by the police," Mary said.

"Yes, I know," Abigail said. "But that is why I am here. Caleb must be warned. And his brother too, if he is here."

Mary shook her head. "Warned about what?"

"The police are going to let Anna go today."

The statement surprised Mary. Had the police held Anna as long as they could without charging her? And what of Henri and Julie?

She forced her thoughts back on the woman in the chair beside her. "How do you know this?"

"I went to see her." Abigail lifted a shoulder in a shrug. "They told me she was busy with paperwork and would be out later today. She may already have been released. I was not told the time, just that there was nothing that could be charged against her." She paused. "I am certain she will come to find Caleb."

"Yes I would imagine she will, seeing as how he is her husband," Mary said. "What is there to warn him about?"

"Mary, you're here." Jake stood in the doorway, a smile on his face. The smile faded when he saw Abigail was there too. "Who is this?"

"This is Abigail," Mary said. "She has something she wants to tell me." She swiveled to look at Abigail. "Now that Jake is here, why don't you tell us what it is that has you so worried? Do you think your sister wants to harm Caleb or Jake?"

Tears now shimmered in Abigail's eyes. "I do not want to believe it, and I do not want to believe that she is capable of harming him. But on Saturday you walked through a workshop that was whole and in use. Today I saw a pile of ashes. How can I be certain my sister did not do that?" A tear slid down her cheek, and she closed her eyes. "I had hope that Caleb might change her."

"Change her?" Jake asked, his brows furrowed. "What do you know about your sister that you're not telling us?"

She shook her head. "I do not know anything, other than you should be careful and watch your brother."

Mary looked pointedly at Jake. "Anna is being released today."

Jake repeated woodenly, "Anna is being released?"

"According to Abigail, yes, she is." Mary returned her attention to Abigail. "Specifically what do you think could happen to Caleb and Jake?"

"To Caleb?" She looked around the waiting room then back at Mary. "He is monitored here, but his wife would make decisions, yes?"

"I believe that's how it would work," Jake told her. "What are you saying she would do?"

Abigail blew her nose. "I do not say something will happen. I hope nothing will happen. I hope your brother will live a long life, and he and Anna will have many beautiful children." She took a deep breath. "But please, watch out for your brother's safety. Do not let her be alone with him right now. And if you need someone to watch him when you cannot be here, I can come sit with him."

"Abigail, why would you say these things about Anna? Do you have proof or evidence that she has set these fires?" Mary asked. "Do you have anything more concrete than suspicions?"

"I have nothing but my fear," she said. "And I hope I'm a foolish woman with foolish fears." She shook her head and abruptly stood. "I should not have come here. Please, just keep watch over Caleb. I do not want anyone to die."

"I plan to," Jake said. "And no one will die on my watch. You can be certain of this." He paused. "In fact, you can tell your sister that. Tell her that Jakob Miller will not be leaving his brother alone again. Not until the arsonist is caught and Caleb is well enough to take care of himself."

Abigail gave Jake a look full of sorrow. "I do not plan to speak to my sister." She turned her attention to Mary. "Please do not tell Anna I was here. She will think I am trying to turn you against her."

"Where will you go now, Abigail?" Mary asked.

She shook her head. "I do not know."

"At least let me be able to find you," Mary said. "Do you have any way for me to contact you?"

Abigail gave her a strange look. "Why do you need to find me?"

"Because I'm concerned about you and your safety. And because you just said you'd be willing to sit with Caleb if we need you to."

"Oh, yes, I have a phone that I can use. Perhaps you could reach me on it."

Mary retrieved her notebook and a pen and handed it to Abigail. "Write the number down, please. I will only use the information if it is necessary."

Abigail did as Mary asked. Then she handed the paper and pen to Mary and walked out of the room without a backward glance.

Mary held the paper, looking down at the number Abigail had written there. She glanced up to see Jake rubbing the back of his neck as if he were trying to massage out some kinks.

"Do you think she's right? Do you think Anna could have set that fire and wished to harm Caleb?" he asked her.

She sighed. "I don't know. Even if Anna did set the fire, that doesn't mean she wanted to hurt Caleb," she said. "Maybe she got angry with him and wanted to destroy something he cared about. Maybe she was doing something in his workshop and accidently dropped a lantern or something."

Jake rubbed his hands together. "Do you think we need to tell the police what Abigail told us?"

"I wouldn't think so," Mary said. "She didn't tell us anything except she was afraid it was Anna. The police already suspect Anna, so I don't see how that gives them any more information. I would assume they already asked Abigail about what she knows when they questioned her the other day."

Jake held out his hand to her. "Caleb is awake. Are you ready?"

Mary squared her shoulders. She wasn't ready to see Caleb. But she was ready for some answers.

CHAPTER FIFTEEN

Elizabeth had fluffed enough pillows in the housewares and décor section of the store to last a lifetime. If she didn't stay busy, she wouldn't be able to keep her mind off the fires and what happened with Caleb and how very close to home this situation had hit.

The doors opened, and she turned around to see Julie Bettencourt step inside. Stifling a gasp, Elizabeth put on a smile and went to greet her.

Before Elizabeth could speak, Julie ducked her head. "I came here to explain what happened the other night, but truly I don't know where to begin." She lifted her eyes to meet Elizabeth's gaze. "I feel like such a fool."

Elizabeth hesitated just a moment and then touched Julie's arm. "Come in, and let's chat. Would you like some coffee or tea?"

Julie followed her without a word. When they arrived at the workroom, she murmured, "Coffee, please," as she sat down on the nearest stool.

Elizabeth made two cups of coffee and placed a cup in front of Julie. "Cream or sugar?"

"Neither." She retrieved the cup and held it in both hands as if warming her fingers. Then she looked at Elizabeth. "I should have told John what I knew on Saturday."

"Would you like to tell him now?" Elizabeth sat across the table from Julie and pulled her phone from her pocket. "I can call him."

"No." Julie shook her head. "It wouldn't matter. It's all come out now. I said what I needed to say to the police after I was detained." She looked down into her coffee cup. "Not arrested. The officers were careful to make that clear to my attorney. Detained for questioning. Though there is still a possible pending charge for who knows what in relation to this whole sorry situation."

When Julie looked up again, there were tears in her eyes. Elizabeth reached for the box of tissues on the shelf behind her and set it on the table between them.

"Oh Elizabeth, what would my dear, sweet husband say if he knew this? I'm just..." She fell into gasping sobs. "I worked so hard to build the business he started into something he would be proud of. So hard. Then... Oh, I'm horrified about all of it."

"Julie," Elizabeth said gently as she hurried to embrace her friend. "Honey, it's going to be okay."

"I don't think it will ever be okay." Julie lifted her head. "All people know is that it looks like I tried to run from the police. That's not at all what happened."

Elizabeth stepped back and then reached to hand Julie another tissue. "That is what it looks like," she conceded. "Especially after your confrontation with Caleb. My sister and Jake Miller saw enough to know that you were angry with him." Elizabeth paused. "And they heard your threat to burn down Caleb's home. Or workshop. Or something."

Julie's eyes widened. "I never made any such threat. Never!" Then she groaned and looked away. "Oh. Of course. I was telling Caleb what someone else said about him."

"And that was an angry threat to burn something down?"

"Yes." Julie looked past her to stare out the door into the store. A moment later, she returned her attention to Elizabeth. "And then she did."

Elizabeth shook her head. "Wait just a minute. You've skipped essential information. Who are we talking about?"

"Anna Miller," Julie said. "I heard her clear as day in the parking lot of Masts' Furniture. I was writing up the ticket for the next drop-off of lumber after leaving an order at Masts'. Then I saw her. Anna was marching through the parking lot with her poor sister just trying to keep up. Oh, but Anna was so angry."

"When was this? And why was she angry?"

"The day before the fire." Julie shook her head. "Anna caught Amos Mast in the parking lot behind the building and gave him an earful about something she heard he told Caleb about her."

"So this was in regards to the argument Amos admits he had with Caleb several days before the fire?"

"Yes," Julie said. "When Anna saw me sitting in the delivery van, she walked over to try to start a fuss with me. I ignored her, of course. I certainly wasn't going to get into an argument over absolutely nothing in a customer's parking lot."

"But you didn't see her set the fire?"

"No. I just heard and saw the threat." She gave Elizabeth a doubtful look. "I'm not sure how seriously they took me. I was sitting in the police station because of what happened Sunday night, so I doubt I had much credibility."

Elizabeth could see the truth in that statement. Still, Julie was well respected in the community.

"Tell me about Sunday night," Elizabeth said. "You went to a lot of trouble trying to not get caught leaving your office."

Julie wiped her eyes and then wadded the tissue into her palm. "I was terrified. All I could think of was to get out of town as quickly as I could."

"Because of what happened in the Masts' Furniture parking lot?"

Her eyes widened. "No. Because of the warning I got on Saturday."

"Warning?"

Julie nodded. "Saturday evening I was at the office doing paperwork. We're not open on Saturdays, so I go in and get things accomplished that I can't do during the week. I heard someone knocking at the loading dock door. When I switched on the camera, I saw it was an Amish woman."

"Anna?"

"Yes. I opened the door. She warned me not to tell anyone about what she'd said to Amos. Then she turned around and left." Julie shook her head. "I didn't tell her that I'd already told Caleb. And at the time I had no idea what had happened to Caleb. It just didn't seem all that threatening. When I went to church on Sunday and heard about the explosion on the Miller farm, I was terrified. If she did that to her own husband, then I had no doubt she would do that to me. So I made a plan to escape without anyone knowing about it." She paused. "That failed miserably."

"Well, it did make headlines," Elizabeth admitted. "You hid in the van and then had Henri come and get you in her wrecker. That's pretty elaborate."

"As I said, I was afraid. That's why I told Henri to be careful not to get caught. But I didn't tell her why I was going to the airport. She didn't know anything about it."

"Julie, Henri took off when she first saw police lights," Elizabeth offered. "Why would she do that if she thought she was just taking you to the airport? You must have told her something about what was going on."

"What? No. I saw a car following us. When it got off at the same exit we did, I panicked. I was afraid it could be Anna. I never noticed flashing lights until we turned onto the dirt road. Were they close to us?"

Elizabeth shook her head. "No, the officer was coming out of the airport."

"Oh, all right. Well, that isn't far from where everything went wrong."

A thought occurred to Elizabeth. "Anna is Amish, Julie. Why would you think she was following you in a car?"

Julie looked at her incredulously. "Elizabeth, would you ever think an Amish woman would knock on your door and practically threaten to burn your business down? If she could do that, why wouldn't I think she'd drive a car too? When someone started following us toward the airport, I thought she'd found me again." Julie paused. "Anyway, I just wanted to come and apologize for drawing you and your sisters into what should have just been my own problem."

"What are you going to do now?" Elizabeth asked.

"Tom Ford, my foreman, has been doing a great job of handling things since I was...well, while I was away, so today I told him he was in charge until he hears otherwise. My lawyer has secured an agreement with the prosecutor to let me leave town as long as I let them know where I am. I will be safe where I am going, because I'm telling no one else."

Elizabeth nodded. "Just one more thing. Why choose Henri to drive you?"

Julie rose and tucked the tissue into her pocket. "That's Henri's story to tell, not mine."

As Julie moved toward the door, Elizabeth followed her. "Thank you for stopping by to tell me this personally."

Julie paused just before she reached the door. "I wish I had told you about Anna when I saw you and John at the coffee shop. Then maybe Caleb would not be in the hospital, and Henri and I wouldn't have ended up on the front page of the local paper."

Elizabeth reached out to hug her once more. "It's going to be okay, Julie. Once the whole story is told, it'll all be fine. You'll see."

She gave Elizabeth a hopeful look. "I really want you to be right, Elizabeth. I just can't have ruined years of hard work over this. I just can't have."

Her voice broke, and tears gathered in her eyes. She retrieved her tissue and dabbed at her eyes as she hurried out the door and into the parking lot.

Elizabeth returned to the workroom, where she'd left her phone. As she reached to pick up the phone and call John, the door opened, and four women stepped inside.

With shoppers in the store and her sisters still not back, Elizabeth tucked her phone into her pocket, put on a smile, and went to see to the customers. As soon as the last one left, she had John on the phone. "Remember that conversation we had with Julie Bettencourt on Saturday?"

"Sure," he said. "Why?"

"She just showed up here and told me her side of what happened Sunday. She also told me about the two run-ins she's had with Anna Miller. She told me she didn't think the officers believed her."

"Last I heard Julie was being released despite the fact that she refused to talk. Apparently her attorney told her to keep her mouth shut and then sprung her."

Elizabeth tried to think back to exactly what Julie had said about talking to the police. "John, what she told me was she told the police what she needed to tell them, or something to that effect."

"Mind hanging on for a sec while I confirm that?"

"Sure. Go ahead."

He put her on hold and then came back a moment later. "Elizabeth," he said, "where is Julie now?"

"I don't know. She said she was leaving town to hide out. Why?"

"I was right. Julie kept her mouth shut until her lawyer told the officers to arrest her or turn her loose." He paused. "Why did she leave jail and go straight to Secondhand Blessings?"

"She said she wanted to apologize for what happened Sunday night."

"No, Elizabeth. She wanted to give her statement to someone before she disappeared, and she chose you."

"Caleb Miller was meant to die in that explosion," Eunice Rohrer repeated to Martha before she took a bite of her cookie and allowed the crumbs to fall into her coffee. "Saul told me that."

"Your husband?"

"Yes, he went over to help when he saw the smoke at the Millers'. We don't live far, and that's what neighbors do." She shook her head. "He said whoever set that fire knew when Caleb would be in the workshop."

"How is that possible?" Martha asked.

"He had a schedule," Eunice said. "Everyone knew Caleb kept certain hours sacred to his work. It did not matter that he now had a wife. He still lived a bit like the bachelor he had been for all those years. Whoever set that fire knew that he was inside."

"What else was on his schedule? Besides working in the workshop during certain hours?"

"I could not say, dear. But perhaps my husband might have an answer." Eunice paused. "Are you an amateur sleuth as well as a baker?"

Martha smiled. "Yes, I guess you could say that I am. My sister and Caleb's brother were at the farm the same day of the explosion."

"I see. Well then, you have a reason to be curious." She paused. "May I give you some advice?"

"Of course."

"As one business owner to the other, be careful not to dig too deeply into this mystery of who is setting the fires. If you get too close to the answer, you might end up being the next one watching your business burn."

CHAPTER SIXTEEN

The doors to the intensive care unit opened. Mary hesitated before stepping inside. Instantly the sounds of machines whirring and alarms beeping surrounded her. Jake nodded toward a door on the right.

"He's in there."

"Okay," Mary managed, taking a step toward him.

"Just to prepare you, he's bandaged up. He won't look like himself." Jake paused. "And he's heavily medicated, so he may be difficult to understand."

"Okay," she said again.

"Are you all right?" Jake asked.

"No," she admitted. "I'm not all right at all. I hate this for Caleb. He belongs at home with…"

She was about to say his wife but that didn't seem appropriate. Not given what she'd just been told by Abigail Byler.

"Anyway, he belongs at home."

"He does, and my goal is to see that he goes home soon." Jake shook his head. "He's in good hands here. I have faith this will happen. Are you ready to go in and see him?"

Mary took a deep breath and let it out slowly. "Yes." She followed Jake into the room, where a bed had been placed in the center. Wires and tubes snaked up, down, and around the figure in the bed.

The whirring and beeps she'd heard outside were louder here. She let out another long breath and pasted a smile on her face as the man beneath the blankets and bandages opened his eyes and focused them on her.

"Hello, Caleb," she said softly.

At first she thought he hadn't heard her. Then the corner of one side of his mouth lifted almost imperceptibly. "Mary."

"Yes, it's Mary," Jake told him. "You asked to see her."

"Mary," he said again. "Thank you for..." He paused as if he'd forgotten what he was going to say. Then, after a moment, he continued. "For coming to see me."

She smiled. "I'm very glad you're feeling up to seeing me."

"Mary," he said, an insistent look on his face. "You find out...who did...this."

"Caleb," Jake asked him, "why do you think Mary can find out?" He looked over at Mary. "He's said it to me several times. I thought it was the medication talking."

"No." Caleb focused on Jake. "Mary will."

"Okay," Jake said. "So you think Mary can find out. How does she do that?"

"Catch before..." Again he paused. This time he dissolved into a fit of coughing that sent the monitors into red zones.

"Okay, buddy," Jake told him. "Settle down, or they'll kick us out."

He battled the cough for another few minutes, and a nurse stepped inside. "Mr. Miller, are you being feisty again?" she asked as if she were addressing an errant toddler. "You're not helping things improve by getting upset." She made some adjustments to the machines and then turned to look at Jake and Mary. "He needs to keep from getting so upset. If you're thinking of talking with him about something that will set him off again, I'd highly recommend you don't do that."

"We're just visiting," Jake said. "I'll see that he remains calm."

She turned to Mary. "And you'll do the same?"

"Absolutely," Mary told her. "I'm only here because he asked me to come."

"All right." The nurse gave them each an appraising look then returned her attention to Caleb. "I'm just outside. You remember how to call me, right? I showed you where the button is."

Caleb ignored her to keep his attention on Mary. Once the door had closed behind the nurse, Mary moved closer to the bed.

"I don't want to upset you, Caleb," Mary said. "If you want to try to talk about this when you're feeling better, I can come back."

"No time...," he said. "Find out before...anyone else hurt." His eyes implored her. "Please."

"Hey, Caleb," Jake said, his tone light. "Why are you telling Mary this?"

"Because she will find who...did this."

Jake looked over at Mary with a questioning look. "Why does he think that?"

She shrugged. "My sisters and I have solved a few mysteries recently. I guess Caleb has heard about it." Mary returned her attention to the patient. "I'll do what I can. I promise."

"Good," he wheezed.

"Can I ask you a question, Caleb?" Mary asked. At his nod, she continued. "What did you and Julie talk about that day at the farm when she was yelling at you?"

"Not...at me," he corrected. "Told me...what she heard." He paused. "She said Anna...argued with...Amos, but she... misheard. Must have."

"Caleb," she said gently. "Did you see who lit the fire that blew up the workshop?"

"No," came out on a strangled breath, and his wracking cough began again. This time the nurse shooed her out before either could protest. Mary returned to sit in the ICU waiting room and wait for Jake.

After a while, he stepped outside with a grim look on his face. "I'm sorry he put you on the spot, Mary. He's been saying things that are, well, that must be the morphine talking."

"It's not a problem, Jake. I don't feel put on the spot. My sisters and I are trying to find some answers."

Jake shook his head. "I'm not sure he knows what he's saying. Yesterday he blamed the Yoders' cows. Said one of them must have turned over the linseed oil into the furnace that was keeping the workshop warm."

She sighed. "Yeah. I see your point, but he did seem coherent."

"He might be," Jake said. "That's the problem. It's hard to know. But just don't think that he's going to remember you were here or that you agreed to anything."

She waited while he took a seat beside her. Then she said, "We should be talking about Caleb and what his prognosis is."

"His prognosis is unknown," Jake said. "He's still here and still hanging in there, so that's good. Thus far he hasn't needed to be transferred to a bigger hospital as was expected, and that's also good." He paused. "There are other things that concern me as a physician, but I'm concentrating on them. I want him well, and that's the bottom line, so I'll take any victory I can celebrate."

"Yes, of course." Mary glanced up at the clock over the door and gasped. "Oh no. Poor Elizabeth. Martha and I have left her alone all afternoon."

She reached for her phone and saw a text from Augie she hadn't notice come in. She opened it.

JUST HEARD FROM SOMEONE WHO BOUGHT ONE OF YOUR PAINTINGS. SHE WANTS SIX MORE FOR A NEW AMISH HISTORY ROOM IN A BRANCH OF THE PHILLY PUBLIC LIBRARY. GRAND OPENING IN 4 WEEKS. WHAT DO YOU SAY? LET ME KNOW SOON.

Mary felt a thread of excitement run through her. Her work in a Philadelphia public library. That would certainly cement her reputation for depictions of Amish life. At the end of the thread was a niggle of doubt. Is that what she wanted?

She pushed aside both feelings and texted Martha.

SO SORRY I TOOK SO LONG. PICK ME UP ANY TIME.

Mary pressed SEND then returned her attention to Jake. "My sisters and I are investigating these fires. Caleb was right about that. But if I can just figure out who or what caused the workshop explosion, I'll be happy."

"I hope you can," Jake said. "Maybe I should be helping you and your sisters."

"No, you should be here with your brother, Dr. Miller," she said with a smile she hoped would reassure him.

"I had a visit from an arson investigator this morning," he told her. "The FBI hasn't yet elected to step in, so a joint task force is being assembled to investigate the fires."

"That's good news, right?"

"I think so." He looked away and then slowly returned his attention to her. "With everyone coordinating their efforts, maybe this person can be stopped before more are hurt." He paused. "Or someone dies."

"I have another question. John asked if I recalled seeing anything or anyone odd or different on the road when we were returning to the farm on Saturday evening. All I can remember is that my eyes were closed most of the time."

Jake cringed. "I might have been driving a bit recklessly."

"Maybe," she said. "But it was an emergency. So I don't suppose you remember which vehicles you passed on the way."

"It was Saturday evening, so the roads were fairly clear once we got near the farm." He stopped talking, as if trying to recall the drive. "Oh, wait a minute. I do remember one." Another pause. "It was a white wrecker. The driver was driving like a maniac, but I figured there must have been an accident somewhere. I remember that he was swerving out of his lane a ways ahead of us, but he was fine when he passed us."

The wrecker Henri drove was white. Mary frowned.

"What? Is there something suspicious about a white wrecker?"

"There might be, especially if you're remembering that the driver was driving fast," she told him.

"Not just fast. Weaving around and, well, anyway, it was enough for me to notice."

John wouldn't have asked if there wasn't some suspicion that the vehicle was involved. Would he?

But surely Henri Sessions wasn't setting fires.

Was she?

"You've got a look that tells me you're thinking about another suspect." He shook his head. "The wrecker driver?"

"I don't know what I'm thinking," she said. "Truly. I don't have enough facts to link any of the suspects with any degree of certainty."

Mary's phone buzzed with another text. She glanced down at it then back up at Jake. "My ride is here."

They stood up together, and Jake walked her down to the hospital entrance. "Thanks for coming. If Caleb does remember you were here, it'll comfort him."

"If he asks again, I can come back. Just let me know."

He reached out and grasped her hand. "Thanks again. It means more than I can tell you."

They exchanged goodbyes, and then Mary hurried out to the parking lot to climb into Martha's car. "How was Caleb?" her sister asked.

"You know, I'm not sure." She filled her in on what had happened. "Of course, Jake says he might not have a clue what he's saying."

Martha shook her head. "That's not very reassuring."

"Jake says it's the morphine."

"And you?"

"Like I said, I'm not sure." She paused. "But I think we have another suspect."

"Who?"

"Henri Sessions."

"Why Henri?"

"John asked about a wrecker driver. Jake says he remembers seeing one driving like a maniac away from the scene."

Martha signaled a left turn. "So if we consider people who were there and had the opportunity, we have three suspects. Anna, Abigail, and Henri."

"Right," Mary said. "Surely that's it, at least as far as the people we know are concerned." She sighed. "At least I sincerely hope so."

"No, we have four," Elizabeth said when they arrived back at Secondhand Blessings and told her the story of their afternoon. "Julie Bettencourt is up to something, and if it's not arson then it's still something worth running from."

"Why do you think that?" Martha asked.

Elizabeth told her everything that happened, including John's warning that Julie had been silent when questioned by the police.

"Okay then," Mary said. "We just have to figure out who or what she's running from. No problem." She paused to consider how she could get to know Julie's situation better. "I know I've been gone all afternoon, but if you're okay without me here, I have an idea."

"Yes, we're fine," Elizabeth said, "but what's your idea?"

"If I tell you, you can't tell John."

Elizabeth frowned at her. "That depends. If you're going to kidnap Julie or something, I'm pretty sure I should tell him."

Mary snorted. "Ha ha. I'm just going to pay a visit to Bettencourt Lumber Supply. It's not like I'll run into Julie there, right?"

"Probably not," Elizabeth said, "but what if you do?"

"I'll figure it out as I go." She paused. "Oh! I know. I'll tell her I need to look at some wood to purchase for frames. Bill is going to make some for me, but I told him to hold off until I know what I want." She shrugged. "Perfect opportunity."

"Why don't you take Bill with you?" Martha suggested. "I'd feel better if you didn't go alone, but I think we've left Elizabeth here by herself long enough, so I should stay with her."

Mary retrieved her phone and called Bill. "Hey there," she said when he answered. "I've got an errand to run that involves the frames I'm going to have you make. Do you mind meeting me at Bettencourt Lumber Supply so I can see what they've got in stock?"

"Actually I do mind," Bill said.

"You do?" She frowned. "Oh, well, okay then. I'm sorry I—"

"Mary," he said quickly. "I'm teasing you. I'd be glad to go with you. I was actually going to check with you in a few days to see if you still wanted them. Since what happened with Caleb and all, I thought the project might be on hold."

"No, it's just that I haven't thought much about it until now. So you'll meet me there?"

"No."

"Bill!" She laughed. "Stop teasing me."

"I'm not teasing you. I won't meet you there." He paused. "I will, however, be at your door in less than five minutes as I happen to be in the area right now. Are you at home or at the shop?"

"At the shop." She ended the call and went to the front window to watch for Bill.

A few minutes later she spied Bill's truck pull up in the parking lot. "My chariot awaits," she called to her sisters and then went out to meet him.

True to his gentlemanly nature, Bill hurried to open her door for her. "You look pretty today, Mary."

"Thank you." She smiled at him as he went around to his side of the truck.

"So what are you thinking for the wood on the frames?" he asked once they were underway.

"I'll know it when I see it." She paused. "I have to confess, I have an ulterior motive for doing this today. Julie Bettencourt is on our suspect list in regard to the fires, and I'm hoping a visit to her store will answer the question of whether she belongs there."

"I think I can handle that," he said. "I guess the plan is to just go in and look at what they've got but keep our eyes open for anything suspicious?"

"I'm hoping you can talk to Tom Ford, the supervisor. Maybe you could come up with some kind of exotic wood you want to see if he can acquire for you. It might take him some time to find out."

Bill offered her that slightly off-center rakish grin. "Leave it to me."

She did, and the plan worked beautifully. After a quick perusal of the small showroom, Bill asked one of the employees if he could speak with Tom. A few minutes later the supervisor escorted them into the massive warehouse that filled most of the building.

Bill let out a low whistle as he surveyed the space. "This is a woodworker's dream right here, Tom. Why don't you show me what you've got that I might be interested in?"

"Sure," Tom said. "Follow me."

Bill fell into step beside him, pausing only to look back at Mary and wink. She hadn't told Bill this part of the plan, but as soon as the men were deep into a discussion of some rare wood from who knew where, she spoke up.

"I'm sorry to interrupt, but where is the ladies' room?"

Tom gave her instructions on the location and went back to talking to Bill. Dedicated friend that he was, Bill seemed more than willing to act the part of interested potential buyer. Mary slipped away unnoticed and moved swiftly toward her destination.

Not the ladies' room but the office she'd spied on the way in. The door with a gold plaque that said JULIE BETTENCOURT, PRESIDENT AND GENERAL MANAGER.

She reached out to turn the doorknob, expecting to find it locked. Instead, it turned easily. A moment later, Mary was inside, the door now firmly closed behind her.

And locked.

CHAPTER SEVENTEEN

Martha watched Mary drive away and then turned back to Elizabeth. "I met Eunice Rohrer today." She paused when Elizabeth didn't respond. "She's the woman who's selling her bakery. I thought I would just go look at the place while Mary was visiting Caleb, but then I ended up talking to Eunice about it."

"Oh." Elizabeth looked up from the shelf she was straightening to meet her gaze. "Well, okay. What were your impressions?"

"It's a busy shop, and Eunice says she has a good clientele, and there's not much to do in the way of improvements. I didn't go inside or look at the kitchen, but the price includes an apartment above."

"Oh," Elizabeth said again on an exhale of breath. "I see. So you could live over the store instead of here with Mary and me if you wanted."

"I could," Martha said. "Or I could lease the apartment out with the hopes it covers my expenses each month."

"You could," Elizabeth agreed and then let silence fall between them. "It sounds like a wonderful opportunity. And Martha, I'm really sorry I forgot to give you the card the day I got it."

"No, it all turned out fine." Martha paused. "Eunice is Amish. We talked about Caleb. She believes someone was targeting Caleb in that fire, and they wanted him to die."

"Why does she think that?"

"Apparently her husband told her that Caleb was a creature of habit, and anyone who knew him would have known where he would be at that time." Martha told her about the rest of the conversation she'd had with Eunice. "As one business owner to the other, she warned me to be careful not to dig too deeply into this mystery of who's setting the fires. She thinks if we get too close to the answer we might end up being the next ones to watch our business burn."

"Huh," Elizabeth said. "I hadn't considered that. But we aren't Amish, so why would they target us? So far it's only been Amish businesses."

"True," Martha said, "but we don't know what the person might do if they think we're getting close to figuring out who they are."

"Then I guess we're going to have to be extra careful," Elizabeth said. "Because I don't intend to stop trying to figure out who's behind these fires. Do you?"

"Of course not." Martha took a breath. "So perhaps we should get Saul Rohrer's insights."

"That's Eunice's husband?" At Martha's nod, Elizabeth said, "Perhaps, although that should probably wait for another day."

Martha looked at her watch and then back at Elizabeth. "Agreed. Once we closed the store and managed to get out to his farm, it would be dinnertime. I doubt arriving at an Amish farm uninvited when the family meal is going on the table would make them want to talk to us."

"So maybe tomorrow," Elizabeth responded, sounding more than a little distracted as she went back to her work arranging quilted pot holders on the shelf. Then she looked up sharply. "Are you leaving us, Martha?"

"Leaving you?" It took a moment to understand the question her sister was actually asking. "If you're asking am I buying the bakery and moving into that apartment, the answer is I don't know yet."

"So you haven't decided on buying the bakery? You might not be leaving here?"

"I haven't," Martha said. "But keep in mind that if your relationship with John or any other man ever heads toward marriage, you'll be contemplating the same question about whether you'll stay here in Mama and Daddy's house. The same goes for Mary."

The startled look on Elizabeth's face and her wide eyes made Martha wonder if she really hadn't considered this possibility.

Elizabeth shook her head vehemently. "I don't think I could ever leave here."

"Not even if you fell in love and got married?"

Elizabeth shook her head again. "Not even then. I mean…" She paused and seemed to be having difficulty gathering her thoughts. "Leave here?"

Martha's mouth fell open. "You're serious, aren't you?"

Elizabeth sighed. "I never expected to enjoy a full house again after Mama died. I liked my peace and quiet, and having you and Mary under that same roof with me was an adjustment, as was working in the store together." She looked into Martha's eyes. "But now I can't imagine it any other way."

"I know you can't," Martha said gently. "It's been wonderful, but nothing lasts forever, Elizabeth."

Tears formed in her sister's eyes. "It's not only our working together, Martha. What's going to happen to the farm if we all move away? If you buy that bakery, you'll end up in the apartment because of how convenient it would be. You'd have to start baking so early in the morning, it'd be so much easier to roll out of bed and just go downstairs, instead of driving in the dark on ice and snow to get there." The tears fell now. "And if Mary marries—and you know she will, eventually—she'll be gone. So how could I marry John and move out? Our house would go to strangers, Mama and Daddy's things would be auctioned off—"

Martha stared at her in disbelief. Elizabeth must be working too hard or not getting enough sleep. Something had her sister going off the deep end. She grabbed a handkerchief from a nearby shelf and handed it to Elizabeth. "Lizze," she said. "Calm down, girl." Who was this, and where was her sensible, levelheaded older sister?

Elizabeth took the handkerchief—tags still attached—that Martha held out to her and wiped her eyes. "I'm sorry, Martha," she said, her voice shaking. She looked around the shop, hoping no one was paying attention to her soggy breakdown. "That was a little dramatic, wasn't it?"

"A little?" Martha's brows were in her hairline. "Are you all right?"

"Yeah," Elizabeth said. "I know I overreacted, but…" How to say this without sounding like a martyr? "I really do feel like I can't leave the farm or the house, or our…*things* here. You know, the kitchen, Mama's flowers, Daddy's workshop, their furniture… it's all so much a part of them.… I grew up here, took care of them here, said goodbye to them here…how can I leave all of it?"

Martha touched Elizabeth's arm. "I know you don't think of John as part of your future yet, because he doesn't share your faith, but don't you think you should consider where you're going with this relationship given what you've just said?"

Elizabeth sucked in a breath. Martha was right. She'd led John to believe that if he were to let God into his life, she'd be open—even eager—to pursue a relationship with him. But to what end? Marriage and moving into his house? After all, he had two children, one still in high school, who wouldn't appreciate their dad selling the home they grew up in and that held memories of their mother.

Could she move out of her parents'—her—house and into John's? If Martha moved to the apartment and Mary married, could she be the one to bring the gavel down on the house that had been in her family for generations? When it came right down to it—could she do it?

Mary sighed and then immediately regretted it. In the quiet of the small space, the sound was deafening.

The office was a walled-off corner of the showroom and jutted out into the warehouse. From what Mary could see, the space was mostly utilitarian in nature with a massive desk taking up most of the room. White metal cabinets lined the wall opposite the windows and provided a surface for a collection of photographs in silver frames and an arrangement of silk flowers in a pewter vase.

There were windows on both sides that presumably looked out onto the activities that went on in the warehouse but were currently blocked by wooden blinds that had been mostly closed.

Tiny rays of light from the warehouse peeked through the slats and cast the room in stripes and shadows. Mary waited for her eyes to adjust to the dim light. Turning on a lamp was too much of a risk.

When she could see well enough to make her way to the desk, she headed in that direction. The plush dark leather chair rolled quietly on a plastic protective pad as she pulled it away from the desk and sat down.

The desk was neatly arranged with a pad that doubled as a calendar and an inbox filled with what appeared to be just a few pieces of mail. Another box, presumably the outbox, held other papers that Mary couldn't read because of the lack of light.

To her right was another stack of papers. Mary retrieved her phone and hit the flashlight icon, blazing the room in light. Instantly, she shut the thing off again.

"That was worse than turning on the overhead lights," she whispered as spots swam in front of her eyes. And for what? So she could see a dentist appointment from last week on the calendar and a receipt from her favorite art store over in Lancaster?

Mary blew out a long breath, more quietly this time. Then she returned the phone to her pocket as her heart rate slowed.

What now? Only then, as she sat at Julie Bettencourt's desk, did the enormity of what she was about to do hit her. She was in someone's office about to go through their desk without their knowledge.

Mary debated. Even though her reasons were good, she couldn't do it.

"Lord, if You want me to find something in here to help stop this person who is preying on innocent businesspeople, then You are going to need to shine a light on exactly what that is. And if You want me out of here without touching a thing, would You make that clear too?" she whispered. "Because You know I can sometimes get ahead of You then look back and wonder where I got lost."

Mary heard voices outside. Tom and Bill were chatting as they walked past the closed door. Though their words weren't completely distinguishable, it sounded like Bill was asking him for plans for some project he had in mind.

"Let's see if I can find them in Julie's office."

That she heard loud and clear. The doorknob rattled. Mary sucked in a breath and dove for the floor beneath the desk.

"That's odd," Tom said. "Julie never locks her office."

Mary crouched tighter into a ball as she heard a key inserted into the lock, and the door opened. Lights blazed.

"She keeps that one in her files," Tom said. "Let me think where. Her desk, maybe."

The breath froze in her lungs. Mary closed her eyes as footsteps drew near. The chair moved. A pair of work boots appeared and then stopped.

"No, it wouldn't be in her desk," Tom said. "It's over here in the filing cabinet. You said you wanted something with a design that wouldn't be difficult to carve into an exotic wood, right?"

"That's right," Bill said. "It can't be something that would make the wood splinter."

"Okay." A file drawer rolled open, and Mary heard the sound of shuffling papers. "Yes, here we go. I think this one would be a good choice. Or that one." He laughed. "I've got a whole file full of plans."

"I'd like to take a look at those, but I wonder if we might be able to go back out into the warehouse and let me see the plans up next to the wood I plan to use. Would that be a problem? I don't want to put you out, what with it being so close to quitting time."

Tom laughed. "We close the showroom at five, but the warehouse workers don't go home until six, so we're good. Let's go out there and see what you like."

The door closed, leaving Mary alone in the office again. This time with the lights on.

She shifted positions to maneuver out of the tight space, and her foot landed on something slippery and banged against the edge of the desk. Again, she froze.

When she was certain no one would be coming back to investigate the noise, Mary reached down to retrieve what she'd slipped on and found a photograph facedown on the carpet. The door opened again, and Mary tucked the photograph into her purse and sucked in a deep breath.

A second later, the lights went off. "Okay," Tom said, "let's go out to the warehouse and see what we can find."

She gave the men just long enough to be gone from the showroom and then braved a brisk walk to the door. Her heart racing, Mary slid the door open just a crack and peered out.

The showroom was empty, so she darted out of Julie's office and raced toward the door to the warehouse. Just as she was reaching for the handle, it flew open.

"Oh!" She stepped backward and then nearly tripped. Bill righted her by grasping both elbows and holding her steady as he stepped inside the showroom and allowed the warehouse door to close behind him.

"I came back to check on you. Do you have any idea how close you were to getting caught under Julie's desk?"

Mary affected an innocent look. "What makes you think I was under her desk?"

Bill removed a cobweb from her hair. "Next time you look for a place to hide, make sure your feet aren't sticking out."

"Oh." She conjured up an image of her red sneakers showing beneath the edge of the desk and giggled. "Well, if I'd been caught, I would've deserved it."

The door opened again. "There you two are," Tom said. "Were you discussing the frame options?"

"Not yet, but I would love to see the selections of wood that you have," Mary said. "I'm thinking of doing a series of paintings I'm calling Barns and Buggies, so I was looking for something with an aged patina for the frames." She looked over at her partner in not-quite-a crime. "What do you think, Bill?"

"I think what the lady wants is what she'll get. Show her that barn wood from Maine that you just showed me. I think she's going to like it."

The remainder of the trip to the lumber store passed quickly with Mary choosing a few lots of beautifully aged barn wood and Bill negotiating the price. "Tomorrow I'll arrange to send you the lumber, Bill, and Mary the invoice," Tom said.

Bill shook his head. "Put it all on my bill and have your delivery man bring it when everything is ready." He paused to look at Mary. "Don't make a fuss," he told her. "I'll send you my invoice when the frames are done."

She grinned. "It's a deal."

Mary waited until Bill pulled out of the store parking lot before she broached the topic of what had just happened. "I couldn't do it, Bill," she told him. "I wanted to go through everything in Julie's desk to try to figure out some kind of link to the fires. Or to find some kind of clue that would tell me she had a good reason to behave the way she has."

Bill slowed to a stop at the red light and then slid her a sideways glance. "I'm proud of you for that. I wasn't sure how I felt about sneaking into an office and looking around. I'm glad you didn't do anything that would make either one of us feel guilty."

"I stopped myself this time." She paused. "I know I get carried away sometimes."

He shrugged. "We all do. Now, do you want to hear what I learned from Tom about his boss?"

Later, back home over dinner, Mary relayed their findings to her sisters. "Tom told Bill that Julie had been working with Caleb on a special project. She'd handled all the ordering and paid all the invoices from her own accounts. Nothing went through the company. The wood arrived at the store under wraps and left the same way, with Julie making the delivery to Caleb personally."

Martha frowned. "That doesn't help. If anything, the mystery deepens. What was Julie up to?"

Mary shrugged. "There's one way to find out." She rose from the table. "I'm going to the hospital to see if I can speak to Caleb again."

An hour later Mary arrived at the door to the intensive care unit and pressed the button to summon a nurse. Soon the same nurse who had rushed her out of Caleb's room before arrived at the door.

"You're here to see Mr. Miller again?" she asked. "He's had a rough afternoon. I'm not sure he's up to visitors."

"I won't be long. I just need to ask him a quick question."

The nurse gave her a skeptical look. Then, reluctantly, she opened the door wide enough to allow Mary in.

The same unpleasant ICU noises assailed her, but Mary ignored them and firmly pressed on toward Caleb's room. She found Caleb by himself.

"His brother isn't here?" Mary asked the nurse, who had followed her.

"No, he went downstairs to get some dinner." The nurse paused to glance over at Caleb then returned her attention to Mary. "Just a few minutes, okay?"

At Mary's nod, the nurse left her alone in the room with Caleb. She took a few halting steps and then stopped to look around.

Everything seemed the same as it had been earlier. Tubes still snaked around, and machines whirred and hummed. But there was something different about Caleb.

She studied his face. Yes, it was there, whatever this change was. Mary just couldn't quite put her finger on what the change might be.

His eyelids fluttered. Then his eyes opened. For a moment he looked up, staring as if trying to make sense of what he saw. Then he turned his head and smiled in her direction.

"Mary," he whispered.

"Yes, it's me." She moved close enough to rest her hand on the bed rail. "The nurse said I could only stay a minute. She said you had a rough afternoon."

He continued to study her, his eyes barely blinking. "All right," he finally said. "I am glad you are here."

Mary smiled. "I need to ask you about something. It's about Julie Bettencourt."

"Julie," he said. "Yes. Nice lady."

"She is a nice lady." Mary paused. "You were working on a project with her, weren't you?" At his slow nod, she continued. "What were you making for her?"

His eyes widened, and he stared past her. "Look, Mary," he told her. "I have never seen such a thing."

Mary followed the direction of his gaze and then returned to looking down at Caleb. "I don't see anything. But that project you were working on with Julie? What was it?"

Caleb tore his attention away from whatever had held it and studied her. "Something special," he told her. "For someone special."

She nodded. "Yes, I know." She thought of the beautiful French easel she'd seen in the corner of his workshop. The one she'd requested he make a copy of for her. "Was it the easel?"

"Easel?" His eyes studied her. "Yes, I will make an easel for you." Then he frowned. "But there was a fire. Anna's easel burned. So I will make two."

"The easel was for Anna?" At his nod, she continued. "What were you making for Julie?"

"*Babywiege,*" came out soft as a whisper. So soft, she wasn't certain she'd heard him correctly.

"Babyveega?" she repeated, sounding the word phonetically because she had no idea of the meaning. Still, she wanted to remember so she could ask Jake. Or Rachel.

He nodded. "Okay." Then she tried again. "How would an Englischer say that word?"

"Babyveega," he repeated, this time more insistent. The beeps on the heart monitor rose. He said it again.

"Yes, all right." Mary smiled. "Thank you, Caleb. That's exactly what I needed to know."

It wasn't, but at least she had something to research. If the word was German, a translation could easily be found. "Jakob will be back soon," she told him. "Do you want me to stay until he returns?"

"Please," he whispered.

"I'll just be right here. You get some rest."

"*Danki.*"

She moved over to the chair nearest the bed. Strategically placed so Caleb could see whoever was seated there, the chair also allowed for a clear view of all the machines to which he was attached.

Just as she was settled on the chair, the door flew open, and Anna Miller marched in.

CHAPTER EIGHTEEN

Anna glared at her. "What are you doing here?"

Mary rose. "I was just here to keep Caleb company until Jake returned."

Anna looked around, then shrugged. "Well, now that I'm here, you can go. I'll take over watching him. After all, he is *my* husband." She folded her arms across her chest. "What do you think it looks like, you alone with my husband?"

Mary stared at Anna in astonishment. *How did it look?* Anna's husband was in critical condition, and that was what she was concerned about?

Mary stood and crossed her arms, matching Anna's stance. She wasn't about to leave their prime suspect alone in the room with her victim. If Anna was the arsonist, it wouldn't take much for her to endanger Caleb's life again, and this time, probably succeed.

"I need to talk to Jake, so I'm just going to wait for him," Mary said through clenched teeth. She sat back down and pointed to the chair next to hers. "Please, sit down."

Anna tossed her head and sat. An awkward silence followed, with neither woman willing to break it.

Mary was debating whether to ask Anna about the clothes on the bed in the dawdy haus when Jake walked through the door. He stopped in his tracks, obviously stunned to see the both of them. Mary wasn't sure which one of them he was more surprised to see. "Mary. Anna. Um…" He shrugged. "Only two of us can be in here at a time."

Anna shot to her feet. "I will go. I see I will get no time with my husband with the two of you here." She turned to Mary. "And now you are not alone with him, as you so obviously wished to be."

Before Mary could recover her wits from that remark, Anna had stalked out of the room.

Jake's mouth dropped open, and he sat in the chair Anna had vacated. "Wow. Just wow." He shook his head, as if to clear it. "What are you doing here?" he asked Mary. "I don't remember you saying anything about coming back this afternoon."

"I hadn't planned on it, but I had a question to ask Caleb," she said. "About something he was working on with Julie. Some special project." She paused. "I told him I would wait with him until you returned."

"But Anna got here first," he supplied.

"Yes. And she made quite an entrance." Mary let out a long breath and then shook her head. "I'm so sorry. I hope none of that upset Caleb."

"I'm sure it did," Jake said, his expression grim, "but that is not your doing, nor should you apologize." He paused. "Tell me about this question again."

She told him about the conversation Bill had with Tom Ford and then relayed her talk with Caleb. "So I thought I might be able to understand what was going on with Julie if I knew what the project was."

"Did he tell you what it was?"

Mary nodded. "I'm not sure of the word. Baby-veega, is what it sounded like."

His eyebrows shot up. "That's what he told you he was working on? A cradle?"

"Babywiege means cradle?"

Her mind reeled as she tried to figure out a connection between all the trouble Julie went to in order to keep her project with Caleb a secret and the behavior she exhibited after the explosion. No good explanation came to mind.

Jake seemed to be trying to do the same. "I thought the cradle Caleb was making was for Anna. Could it have been for Julie? And if that's the case, why would she show up at his shop yelling about burning his place down?"

"It makes no sense."

Then Mary remembered the photograph in her purse.

"Look." She held out the picture to show Jake. "It's exactly like the one Caleb was working on. I found it under Julie's desk. I wasn't thinking and stuck it in my purse. I'll return it to her as soon as I can."

He nodded. "Yes, that's the same cradle."

"What that has to do with everything else going on is another mystery." Mary shrugged. "Anyway, the nurse said Caleb had a difficult afternoon. Has his prognosis changed?"

"No, it's the same." Jake sighed. "Is there any more news about the investigation?"

"No," she said. "We're just working on gathering facts and— we hope—eliminating suspects." She picked up her purse and stood. "Well, it's time for me to go home."

Jake rose to his feet and reached for the door handle then paused to look back at her. "Thank you for all you're doing to get to the bottom of this. I appreciate it, and I know Caleb would tell you the same if he could."

"I hope we'll have an answer soon."

Jake nodded. "So do I. Before another building burns."

On Tuesdays Secondhand Blessings opened its doors from ten till two. Once closing time arrived, Martha was quick to lock up.

They had voted last night to work on paring down the four suspects. "Since Henri is the only one we haven't made contact with," Mary said, "I vote we pay her a visit at the garage today."

After a quick sandwich lunch, they piled in Elizabeth's car and headed toward Chester's Autos. Mary decided it was as good a time as any to bring up the elephant in the room.

"Martha," she ventured, "have you given any more thought to buying that bakery?"

Martha twisted her neck to see into the back seat, where Mary was. "I have," she said. "I've been thinking about all the advantages." She counted on her fingers. "I'd have more money to travel, so I could see the kids more often, and I could go on vacations like the ski trip they wanted to take last Christmas." She held up another finger. "I love to bake, and this would let me do it full-time." She held up a third finger. "I could direct my customers to Secondhand Blessings, and you could direct your customers to me. And…" Another finger. "My own business, run the way I want, organized the way I want, with the hours I want."

Mary could see Elizabeth's troubled face in the rearview mirror. "I didn't know you were unhappy with the way we run the shop," Elizabeth said. "Are you really that dissatisfied?"

Martha was quiet for a moment or two. Mary fought to keep from repeating Elizabeth's question. It had taken her some time, but she'd finally realized that when Martha was quiet after being asked a question, it didn't mean she hadn't heard or was ignoring the question. It meant she was holding up the possible answers in her mind and going through them one by one until she landed on the right one. More than once Mary had wished she had such a filter herself. Openness and candor were laudable at times, but Mary had hurt others' feelings more than once because she'd blurted out an answer she hadn't quite thought through.

When Martha answered, she spoke slowly. "No, it's not that I'm dissatisfied." She sighed. "You know I got a business degree in college, and I was thinking of opening up a restaurant. Then I met Chuck, and even though I finished the degree, I decided marrying him was what I wanted, not a business. And I've never regretted that decision. We had a lovely, lovely life."

"You did," said Mary. "And you still do. I can't imagine your life without Craig and Trish and Kyle and the grandkids."

"Oh, I would never, ever regret anything I did that led to them," Martha reassured her. "But sometimes, when I have a moment to dream, I think…could I have done it? Could I still do it? Do I have what it takes to be excellent at something, and follow through with it?"

"But you are excellent at baking," Elizabeth protested. "We practically sell out every day at the shop."

Martha was quiet for another moment. "I know I'm good at it," she said. "But I also know that at one point in my life I could have been better." She looked down at her lap. "Baking is one of those things I can do with my eyes closed. It comes naturally to me. I can accomplish with no effort what it takes others much effort to accomplish."

Mary knew this was true. But she also knew that Martha wasn't being egotistical. She was sharing something that worried her. So Mary stayed quiet and let Martha continue at her own pace.

After another moment, Martha said, "I just sometimes wonder if I've squandered the natural talent God has given me. I've never challenged myself to go beyond what's comfortable. I've never had to work at it. I always quit before it gets hard."

She looked up and back at Mary. "And so I wonder…what could I accomplish if I really tried? If I put some effort into it?"

Elizabeth reached over and took Martha's hand. "Martha," she said, "if what you've done so far isn't trying, I can't even imagine what you could do if you put your mind to it. And"— Mary could hear her oldest sister choke up a little—"if you feel God is asking you to challenge yourself…then we wouldn't stand in your way, would we Mary?"

"Of course not," Mary said, feeling a few tears spring to her own eyes. Secondhand Blessings without Martha? It was hard to imagine such a thing.

Elizabeth pulled into the lot at Chester's, and the sisters got out of the car. Mary turned around, looking for Chester, and finally spotted him bent over a car in one of the bays. "There he is," she informed her sisters, pointing. "Let's go."

Chester must have sensed them coming, because he straightened up and met them at the door of the bay, wiping his greasy hands on his coveralls. "Hello, ladies," he said. "What have I done to deserve a visit from all three Classen sisters at once?" His voice had an edge to it, as if it wasn't an especially pleasant occurrence for him.

Elizabeth took the lead. "We've come to talk to Henri. Is she around, and can you give her a few minutes to talk?"

Chester turned red and looked down at the ground. "Well, um...you see...Henri isn't here."

"Will she be in later today?" asked Mary.

"No," said Chester. His demeanor changed, and he looked squarely at her, folding his arms across his chest. "I fired Henri this morning."

CHAPTER NINETEEN

Elizabeth cajoled Chester into giving them Henri's address. A short while later, they pulled up in front of a cozy duplex on the outskirts of New Holland.

To Mary's surprise, Henri answered on the first knock. "I've been expecting at least one of you." She shrugged. "Looks like I got all three. Come on in."

They entered into a sparsely decorated living area. A television balanced on what appeared to be a nightstand from an antique bedroom set. Placed in front of it was a pale blue sofa and two matching floral chairs. Henri took her place in one of the chairs and nodded for the sisters to be seated on the sofa.

"What do you want to know?" she asked when they'd settled.

"Did you set the fires at the Amish businesses?" Mary blurted out.

"Okay, well, I guess we're getting right to it," she said. "No, I did not. Nor do I know who did."

"Can you prove that?" Martha asked.

"I have records that would show where I was at the estimated times the fires happened." Henri waved her hand. "I've already shown the police all that."

"What kind of records?"

Henri looked like she was about to cry. "When the cops asked that question I didn't want to show them, because I didn't want to lose my job. Then I lost my job." She took an unsteady breath. "I loved my job at Chester's, but he doesn't pay me nearly enough, so I started a side job."

"What kind of side job?" Elizabeth asked.

"Driving," she told them. "There's a big market for drivers for the Amish. I just cashed in on it, or at least my little slice of it. Had a good thing going too. I would drive them around, or I'd run errands for them. Like if somebody needed something from the grocery store but was housebound, I'd pick it up and bring it to them."

"Why would you hesitate to tell the police that?" asked Martha, ever practical. "Chester can't keep you from having another job in your spare time, can he?"

"No, he can't," Henri said. "As long as I never took work while I was clocked in at the garage." She looked down at her lap. "It all worked great until my car broke down." Her chuckle held no humor. "A mechanic with a car that won't run. Ironic, isn't it?"

"It is," Elizabeth said. "And I imagine that would put a damper on your side job."

Henri looked at her. "Chester let me drive the wrecker back and forth from home to work until I could get my car fixed. What he didn't know was I couldn't afford the parts to fix it. I've been a little strapped for cash lately. Credit card bills and such. I took the side job to help me to pay them off."

"So you had to stop the driving job, then?" Mary asked.

"I should have," Henri told her. "If I had, I wouldn't have lost my job at Chester's when he found out I was using the wrecker for unauthorized use. But I couldn't stop. I mean, I kept getting calls. People needed to get places or have things delivered, and they didn't care whether I showed up in my car or Chester's wrecker, you know?" She paused. "So I started taking just an odd job here and there. Only the ones that paid well. Chester said the loaner was just for me to drive to and from work, but I was hoping—foolishly, I see now—that maybe he wouldn't find out."

"It is kind of wishful thinking to think he wouldn't find out you're driving a Chester's Autos wrecker around picking up Amish people in this tiny town," Martha said. Mary silently congratulated her sister for not sounding like she thought Henri had used very bad judgment. "But he did find out," she continued briskly. "And now you're in even more trouble than a lost job. I'm going to be very frank with you, Henri. The three of us are looking into the mystery of who is setting these fires, and we have a list of four suspects. You're one of them."

"And the other three?"

"Anna Miller, her sister Abigail, and Julie Bettencourt."

Henri sat back and let out a long breath. "I know all of them," she said. "They've all called me for a ride lately."

"We know about Julie, but Abigail and Anna too?" Martha asked. "When?"

"And when have you driven Julie other than the other night leaving her office?" Elizabeth added. "Just so we have the full picture."

"That was the only time I've driven Julie. She wanted to fly under the radar, so to speak, and get to the airport without anyone knowing she was leaving." Henri blew out another long breath. "That didn't work out like we hoped."

"And the sisters?" Martha supplied. "Did you drive them often?"

"Often enough," Henri said. "I would have to check my records to see just when that was."

"Would you be willing to let us look at your records?" Mary asked. "We might be able to establish some kind of timeline or pattern."

Henri appeared to be ready to say yes. Then she shook her head. "My lawyer told me not to turn over anything to anyone, so I'm sorry. I can't do that. I'm not even sure if I should be talking to you now."

"Your lawyer?" Elizabeth asked. "Why do you need a lawyer?" She paused. "And how can you afford one?"

"Julie is paying for it," Henri said.

"Is she now?" Elizabeth exchanged looks with Mary then returned her attention to Henri. "What was your assignment the night you drove Julie?"

Henri clasped her hands together. "I was supposed to drive in through the alley, wait for her with my lights out by the loading dock, then get her to the airport. Originally we were set to meet earlier, but when I got there, there was a note saying to come back later."

"Did you think that was odd?" Mary asked.

"I thought all of it was odd, Mary." She shook her head. "'Wear a hat so you aren't recognized. Approach the lot without lights. I'll jump out of the van and climb in, so make sure your dome light doesn't come on.' Well, that one I forgot to do. The whole thing was like something out of a movie."

Mary frowned. "Didn't Julie wonder about the fact that both sides of your vehicle had Chester's Autos written on it? That kind of negates any ability to remain anonymous."

"If she did, she didn't mention it, and besides, it was dark." Henri leaned forward and rested her palms on her knees. "Look, ladies, you're assuming I asked questions I didn't ask. When I did these side jobs, all I needed to know was where to pick you up and where you needed to be dropped off. I was to pick Julie up at the loading dock and drop her off at the airport. She was going to pay me very well. That's all I needed to know."

"But once you got near the airport, the plan changed again," Martha said.

"It did. Julie saw you all following us and started yelling for me to turn left instead of going straight to the passenger drop-off. I kept telling her that it was a dirt road, but she insisted. Then she said she would double my fare. So I did it."

"And ended up at the police station," Mary said. "I'm just glad you pulled over right away and didn't start a high-speed chase."

Henri looked at her incredulously. "Come on, Mary," she said. "This is Bird-in-Hand, not Hollywood. But you're right. When you're in the middle of a situation like that, there's not a lot of rational thinking going on. If there was, I wouldn't have gotten into the situation in the first place, you know?"

"So you did the right thing then," Mary conceded, "but why not own up to what was going on when the cops stopped you? Was Julie paying you well enough to go to jail for her?"

Henri looked her in the eye. "Yes, she was."

"Is she still?" Elizabeth asked.

"I don't follow."

"Is she still paying you to keep quiet?"

"I think we're done here," Henri said. "I've told you what you came to hear, and that's all I'm saying. I won't talk about Julie or, for that matter, your other two suspects. They're all good customers, and I can promise you I never drove one of them anywhere with the purpose of setting a fire."

"How do you know?" Martha asked.

Henri opened her mouth as if she might respond, then clamped it tight. After a moment, she shook her head. "I guess I can't know that with one hundred percent certainty."

Elizabeth held up her hand. "Henri, have you heard that the last fire that was started has elevated this spree of arson to a federal case?"

"How so?" she asked.

"The arsonist set fire to a building that was a business connected to a home. Back in the home, they were holding services." Elizabeth paused. "Church services. So it became an attack on a church, which is a federal offense, and a hate crime. It's very possible local law enforcement will be replaced by the FBI soon."

"I doubt the Feds will be as nice as the locals," Mary told her. "If you're hiding something, they're going to find out about it, and they won't go easy on you."

"Are you trying to frighten me?"

"Yes," Mary said. "I am trying to frighten you. By telling you the truth. Now why don't you tell us the truth, Henri?"

Henri rose. "Now we're definitely done here. I'm going to have to ask you all to leave."

Elizabeth and Martha rose and walked toward the door. Mary lagged behind to try one last time. "I don't think you did anything wrong, Henri," she told her. "But I think someone used you to commit crimes. Specifically to set those fires."

"I told you, I don't have a clue if that's true."

"I know." Mary paused. "But if not knowing bothers you, then please help us."

Henri looked away for a moment then returned her gaze to Mary. "Anna Miller and her sister were my best customers. Like I said, I only drove Julie once."

"Where did you drive the sisters?" Mary asked.

"All over," she said. "Abigail went to Lancaster more than Anna did, but they both preferred riding with me to taking the buggy for anything other than visiting friends. Anna said they'd take the buggy when they were visiting because the neighbors expected it."

Mary nodded. "Would you take them to the same place every time in Lancaster?"

"Pretty much. There were a couple of central spots where I would let them off—over by the hospital and on the other end of town by the bus station. Sometimes I had both riding, but most times it was one or the other. I would pick them up later at a time we decided on before they left my car. They always had shopping bags and whatnot, so I assume they walked all over." She paused. "So you probably couldn't determine where they went by where I let them out."

"Did you ever drive either of them here to New Holland?"

Henri sighed. "No. But then, I'm not the only ride in town."

Mary nodded. "Okay. Well, is there anything else you're thinking of right now that you need to tell us?"

"Just that I never picked Anna up at the farm. Caleb didn't like that, or so she told me. She always took the buggy into town and parked it out of sight somewhere close to the garage. Then I'd go get her and take her wherever she wanted to go."

"What about Abigail?"

She shook her head. "Abigail didn't care that Caleb didn't like her taking off in a vehicle. He would come out of the workshop or from the field—depending on the time of day, because Caleb had his schedule—and he would fuss at Abigail for being worldly. Didn't bother her a bit. In fact, she'd laugh at him."

"That doesn't sound like the behavior of a woman who's dependent on someone for a place to live."

"Anna wouldn't have made her leave, and she knew it." Henri paused. "Those two were thick as thieves, except when they weren't."

Mary gave her a sideways look. "What do you mean?"

"There were times when they would chatter real quiet-like in their Amish language, and then other times the tension was really thick between them and they wouldn't talk to each other at all." She shook her head. "They're an interesting pair."

"I haven't been around either very much," Mary said. "Is Abigail's temper as bad as Anna's?"

Henri laughed. "I've never seen Abigail mad at anyone. Anna would start ranting and raving, and Abigail would sit back and laugh."

Mary said goodbye and joined Elizabeth and Martha on the front sidewalk.

"Well," Elizabeth said as they made their way back to the car, "that was certainly interesting. I feel like we got a lot of information, and at the same time I feel like we got nothing."

Mary couldn't help but agree. They didn't know Henri all that well. How far could they really trust her?

CHAPTER TWENTY

Mary's phone rang, wakening her from a sound sleep. She'd finally dropped off at midnight and had been dreaming ever since of trying to capture buggies and barns on canvas only to have them slide off and disappear before the paint was dry.

She glanced at the clock. A quarter to three.

Oh no. No. No.

The phone was charging on her desk, so she scrambled across the room to reach it, stubbing her toe on the corner of her nightstand in the process. Her heart racing, Mary had already started conjuring up all sorts of horrible reasons for her phone to ring in the middle of the night.

"What's happened?" she asked in lieu of hello.

Nothing but soft whimpering sobs could be heard. Mary's panic went into overdrive as she scrambled for her reading glasses so she could see the name of the caller.

She dropped them twice before nearly jabbing her eye while putting them on. All the while she imagined the horrible things that could have happened to one of her children or grandchildren. Finally she got a clear view of the phone.

Jake Miller.

"Jake?" Mary sat on the floor, gripping the phone, her heart still racing. "What's happened? Is it Caleb?"

"Caleb's in a coma. They don't think he'll wake up."

"Oh Jake," she said softly. "I am so sorry. So very sorry."

Then she listened to him cry until he could speak again. "I'm sorry. I woke you up. I just…"

"Don't be sorry, Jake. You did the right thing to call me. Do you want me to come to the hospital? Or wherever you are?"

"No," came out on a shuddering breath. "I don't know where I'll be, but I won't leave him again. It happened when I left him, Mary. He was fine, and then he wasn't. It was that fast."

Mary braced herself for what she knew would come next.

"Anna," he said with icy steel in his voice. "I bet she came back and did something while I was gone."

"You don't know that," she hurried to say. "You're a doctor," she reminded him. "I know this is your brother, but you have to keep your wits right now, okay? Caleb needs you to keep your wits right now."

Jake heaved another shuddering sob before clearing his throat. "Yeah," he managed. "I know. I will."

"Okay, don't let your emotions cause you to say or do anything you'll regret." She paused. "Are you sure you don't want me to come and just sit with you wherever you are?"

"I'm sure."

"Okay." Mary shifted positions. "Then tell me how I can help."

"I don't know." He was quiet for a moment. "Maybe I'll know tomorrow, but tonight I don't know. I just need to talk right now."

"Okay," she said again. "Then I'm just going to sit here and be quiet and let you talk or cry or whatever you need to do."

"Thank you, Mary." He paused. "Remember when Caleb used to follow me around when he was a kid? There was that time..."

And so it went until the purple night sky was teasing golden sunrise at the horizon. Only then did Jake finally run out of memories. The silence fell between them, and Mary allowed it.

Finally, she gently called his name.

"It's a new day, Jake, and His mercies are new again. Get some sleep, and call me if you need anything, all right?"

"Thank you, Mary," he said. "I will."

Then he was gone. Only then did Mary allow herself to hang her head and cry for him.

The next day all three sisters were in the shop when Rachel came in with Hannah and Phoebe, who was carrying a basket covered with a cloth. Mary greeted them when they got to the front counter.

"Hello, ladies," she said. "Have you got something for us this morning?"

Phoebe was practically jumping up and down, she was so excited. Elizabeth came up to her and hugged the young woman and received a hearty squeeze in return. Phoebe, who had Down syndrome, was never stingy with her hugs. Martha was right behind Elizabeth, waiting her turn.

"We do have something!" Phoebe said, her face glowing. "Aunt Leora showed us how to make candles, and we want to see if you can sell them here." She took the cloth off the basket, and Mary saw a dozen or more candles in a variety of colors, shapes, and sizes.

"Those look beautiful, Phoebe," she said, reaching in and pulling out a fun cupcake candle. She held it to her nose. "Mmm, vanilla, right?"

"Yes," said Hannah, Phoebe's younger sister. "We also have apples and cinnamon, pumpkin spice, and pecan praline, because we think people might start wanting fall scents and colors very soon."

Phoebe clapped her hands. "And we also have them in jars, and Hannah is learning how to carve them." She frowned at Hannah. "I keep telling her to hurry up and learn so we can sell them." Then she squeezed Hannah's arm. "She thinks she needs more practice, but I think the ones she has done are pretty enough to sell right now."

Hannah blushed. "I hope to have some ready in a few days for you." She turned to Martha. "Do you think they will sell?"

"I certainly do," Martha said, taking each candle out of the basket and laying it out on the counter. Besides the cupcake candles there were one- and three-wick candles in mason jars, taper candles, votives, and pillars. "You get me as many as you can make, because I know these will fly off the shelf."

While Martha and Hannah discussed price and profit margin and Phoebe listened in, Rachel took Mary and Elizabeth aside.

"Have you heard Caleb Miller is in a coma?" she asked them.

At Mary's and Elizabeth's nods, she continued. "Our community is having a gathering to support Anna and Abigail during this very difficult time. We will have it tonight at our house, and I would like for you to come." She touched Mary's arm. "I have invited Jakob. He needs family now, and so we are hoping this will be a reason for reconciliation between Anna, Abigail, and him."

Mary smiled at her. "That's a wonderful idea, Rachel. Of course we will all be there."

"Thank you," said Rachel. "Please come at seven. We will have plenty of food, so come hungry."

"We'll be there," Mary repeated. "And we'll be praying, of course, that Caleb wakes up."

"Rachel," Elizabeth said hesitantly, "would you mind if I didn't come? I think I'll go to the hospital and offer to sit with Caleb so Jake can come. I'm sure he wouldn't want to leave Caleb alone."

"That is very thoughtful of you, Elizabeth," Rachel said. "I would be very grateful if you would do that for Jakob. We would like him to know that his community supports him. After all, he is not shunned by us."

"That's what I was thinking," said Elizabeth. "I'll try to get him to come."

That afternoon a friend of Martha's was taken to the hospital for an emergency appendectomy, so Martha took Elizabeth there and visited her friend. She and Mary would pick Elizabeth up after they finished at Rachel's.

Mary and Martha arrived at Rachel's just before seven and joined the Amish community first in silent prayer for Caleb and then in fellowship as the women shared their delicious cakes, cookies, pastries, and pies. Jake had yet to make an appearance.

It was sprinkling outside, so Mary sat in Rachel's parlor waiting for Martha to get their coffee and join her. As usual, every inch of the room gleamed, from the polished floor to the sparkling-clean windows that had been thrown open to the breeze.

Mary thought sadly of the blackened pile of lumber and ash that was once Caleb's workshop. She thought of the cradle he had been lovingly creating for Julie but with hopes of some-day needing his own, and of that beautiful French easel that would never see paint or canvas.

And the sweet and gentle man who was now fighting for his life and might not ever need his own cradle.

Tears came to her eyes, and she reached into her purse to retrieve one of Mama's handkerchiefs to dab them away. The handkerchief held traces of Mama's favorite perfume, which brought more tears.

The cause of the fire at Caleb's workshop was still unknown. From the murmurings heard around town, some thought the explosion and fire was an accident. After all, there were plenty of combustibles in a workshop and ample fuel once a fire began.

Others thought otherwise. No one who'd spoken to Mary had pointed fingers, but the question of Anna's involvement hung silently in the air each time the subject of the fire came up.

The task force had only just begun investigating. Even so, the threat of federal agents coming in was still spoken of.

Mary heard voices in the doorway behind her. She turned to see Anna and Abigail coming her way, with Martha close

186 | MYSTERIES of LANCASTER COUNTY

behind, cups in hand. The two Amish sisters passed by Mary without speaking and settled in chairs across the room.

Martha sat down beside Mary and handed her one of the cups. "I guess I'm not surprised they're not too keen on talking to us," Mary said.

"I wonder how Anna is really holding up," Martha said.

Mary took a sip of her coffee. "I would guess not well," she said. She lowered her voice. "Especially if she had something to do with Caleb's condition. She's got to be looking over her shoulder all the time." She sighed. "I hope that's not the case, and I hope that the community rallying around her like this is helpful to her."

"It's hard," Martha said. "I pray she feels God holding her like I did."

Mary reached over to squeeze her sister's hand. A widow of just a few years, Martha was so strong and had walked out her widowhood in faith that God was just and fair even when He seemed to be neither.

Mary heard a familiar voice and turned to see Jake walking into the parlor. His expression softened when he spied Mary watching him but became guarded again as a pair of Amish men walked over and engaged him in conversation.

She recognized one of them as Mr. Yoder, Caleb's neighbor, and could tell the topic was more serious than condolences by the way the men spoke. After a few minutes, Jake nodded and shook their hands. Mr. Yoder and his companion went outside where the covered food tables were.

Jake walked over to join Mary and Martha. Dark circles ringed his eyes, and he looked as if he hadn't slept in a week.

To Mary's consternation, Anna and Abigail rose and crossed the room to meet him.

Anna frowned at him. "I do not want you here."

Abigail's expression echoed her sister's words. "You do not belong here."

"You'll have to deal with me eventually," he said evenly to Anna, ignoring Abigail. "The truth needs to come out. Are you prepared for that?"

Mary touched Jake's sleeve. "Jake," she said softly. "Not now."

"I am not prepared to lose my husband," Anna snapped. "And that is all I can consider at the moment."

Martha gave Jake an apologetic look. "I'll just get Anna over to the Yoders. They're going to see her and Abigail home."

Mary focused on Jake. "Why did you say that to her?" she asked after Martha and the other two women were gone.

"It was arson," Jake said. "You and I were there less than two hours before the explosion. Both of us walked through the workshop. There was no indication of any sort of imminent danger in there."

He was right. But his timing was awful.

"She knows more than she's saying," he added.

"She's not saying anything, because she's in shock," Mary told him. "And I find it a little troublesome that you would bother her like that when her husband is lying in a coma."

"A husband she doesn't seem to care about," he snapped. "And Caleb was my brother a whole lot longer than he was her husband."

"Jake, that's enough," Mary said firmly. "Let's remember where we are."

Looking properly chastised, he gave a curt nod. "Yes, you're right." He touched her arm. "Please forgive me. I have no excuse for my behavior. And I'm frustrated because the Amish are closing ranks and not speaking to the fire investigators."

Mary put her hand on his arm. "There is nothing to forgive. You have every reason to be upset."

Jake shook his head. "I appreciate that, Mary."

Mary squeezed his arm. "Now that we've gotten that settled, Jake, if there's anything we can do to help, please just say the word."

"You all have already done so much. Elizabeth is sitting in the hospital with Caleb so I can be here." He nodded toward the window. "Let's go outside."

"Of course."

The rain had stopped, and raindrops glistened on leaves and shook down in a rainbow of light and sparkles with every breeze that slipped past.

Mary walked with him to the driveway where just about a dozen buggies and two cars remained.

Martha came toward them. "I think I'll head to the hospital and then home. Will you be coming with me, Mary, or will you get a ride?"

Jake waved at her. "Don't worry, Martha. I'll see that Mary makes it home safe. I just have something I want to discuss first."

"That's fine," Martha called. She veered off toward her car.

Mary returned her attention to Jake. "So you were saying that the fire investigators are having trouble getting the Amish they wish to interview to speak with them. That's odd, because there's always been cooperation between first responders and the Amish."

"It doesn't surprise me," Jake said bitterly.

"I don't understand. There wasn't an issue with this before the fire at Caleb's place. At least not that I heard about."

"Odd as it sounds, now that Caleb is in danger of dying, there's a feeling of protectiveness toward Anna," he said. "She's not from the area, but Caleb was well loved and she was his wife, so that's enough for most of them to feel certain she couldn't have caused any harm to her husband. And enough to think that I might have."

"Seriously? They suspect you? Why would anyone think you did it? What purpose would you have to set fire to your brother's workshop?"

"I was seen at Caleb's just hours before the workshop exploded."

"Who saw you there?" She shook her head. "If they saw you there, they probably saw me there too. Why not think I did it? This is ludicrous."

"Samuel Troyer and his youngest son were working in the field down the road. They saw us arrive, leave, and then turn back around to follow Anna home."

"So?"

"So Anna had just come from the Troyer home after spending a few hours letting them know what transgressions needed to be dealt with in the community." He paused. "According to Samuel, chief among her concerns was Caleb's prodigal brother who walked away from the faith but wouldn't leave her husband alone."

CHAPTER TWENTY-ONE

Mary frowned. "Anna complained about you to the Troyers? But you hadn't even come to the farm at that point yet. She'd never even met you."

"I don't think that matters," Jake said. "Yesterday I went out to the farm to see what needed doing and found a neighbor there by the name of Saul Rohrer plowing the field."

"Yes, I've heard of him," Mary said.

"He spent a lot of time with Caleb and knew a whole lot more about how he and Anna ended up married than my brother ever told me about. According to Saul, Anna's mother was against the wedding because she felt the Amish community Anna was marrying into wasn't strict enough and would lead her astray."

"How did Caleb persuade Anna to marry him?"

"Saul said Anna thought she could show Caleb the way of life she felt God called him to, and then she and Caleb could lead the community back to 'the right path.' He said she's been going to every meeting and quilting bee and sewing circle there is and also going to people's houses telling them how they need to give up the trappings that keep them from the life God expects them to live."

"Wow." Mary thought of Caleb and Anna's musty, dusty house, with no aromas of food cooking. No wonder. Anna didn't have time to take care of a house if she was busy going to every meeting and visiting every house in the community.

He shook his head. "Apparently Anna's father overrode her mother. He told Caleb that he and his wife are both in poor health, and he feared what life would be like for Anna if they died without her being married."

"But he wasn't worried about Abigail?" Mary shook her head. "I'm sorry. I shouldn't have said that. I'm just sort of baffled by all of this."

"I think he's still looking for a husband for Abigail," Jake said. "What was important to him was that Caleb is a faithful man. He knew that if Caleb promised to love and cherish Anna till death parted them, he would do just that." Jake paused to wipe his eyes. "That's my kid brother. He loves big, and he keeps his promises. He's always been a better man than I am. Her father was right."

The sound of a car engine refusing to start interrupted them. Mary stepped back to turn and look toward Martha's vehicle. The sound rose up again.

"It sounds like your sister needs some help." He walked over to motion for Martha to open the hood. A few minutes later he made his diagnosis. "It's your battery. I can take it out and get a replacement for you. I'll drop you and Mary off and go handle it."

"No need," Martha said. "I've got roadside assistance. Just let me make a call."

A few minutes later, she ended the call. "We're in luck," she said. "They're sending someone out with a battery. They said it would take less than ten minutes."

"That's good news," Mary said.

"No battery trouble at all would be even better," Martha said. "But yes. The local supplier of batteries is Chester's Autos, so they're not far at all."

"Why is he still here?"

Mary turned to see Anna walking toward them with her sister on one side and Mr. Yoder on the other. As they neared the driveway, she broke off from the other two and headed toward Jake with a look of fury on her face.

"I told you to leave," she snapped. "You never do what you are supposed to do. If you did, you would be living the life God wants you to live and not breaking your brother's heart."

"Anna, hush." Abigail moved to stand between her sister and Jake. "I am sorry. She is upset."

"As am I," Jake said, his eyes steely and his tone clipped.

"You did this. You did this to my husband." Anna shrieked and landed on the ground in a puddle of skirts. "This whole community needs the fear of God. My husband refused to shun his brother and brought the wrath of God on himself."

Abigail knelt beside her and tried to offer comfort. Mr. Yoder stood back with a look on his face that told Mary he wished he was anywhere else but here.

"I did no such thing," Jake said. "You of all people know this is true."

"Ben," Mrs. Yoder called, "what is this fuss?"

"The woman is distraught," he said to his wife. "Her sister is tending to her, and then we can take her home."

Mrs. Yoder switched to German, which Mary did not speak, but the tone was unmistakable. Anna Miller's behavior was unacceptable, and Mr. Yoder should somehow do something about it.

"Perhaps we should leave now," he said to the ladies. "You will be more comfortable at home."

But Mr. Yoder's words only made Anna yell louder. Finally Abigail was able to convince her sister to calm down enough to stand. When she was on her feet again, Anna swayed until Abigail caught her.

"We should leave," Mr. Yoder repeated. "Now, before there is any more trouble."

This time Abigail coaxed her sister all the way to the buggy before Anna stalled and turned around to face Jake. "You will say nothing more," Mrs. Yoder barked. "Get in now, Mrs. Miller."

The harsh words must have shocked Anna into motion, for she did as the older woman said and quickly disappeared into the depths of the plain black buggy. Mr. Yoder, who had wisely tarried while the women handled the irrational newlywed, gave Jake an apologetic look.

"She is not herself," he said.

"I wouldn't be so sure about that," Jake said. "And I won't make any secret of the fact that I believe she's responsible for my brother's condition. I know what your own eyes have witnessed, and so do you. It's not a big leap to go from what we've both seen to what happened last Saturday and draw the conclusion that the bride wished to be a widow."

Mr. Yoder bowed his head and then, after a moment, lifted it again. "It is as you say," he said softly. "But the proof? That is another thing, Jakob."

"I'll get proof," he told Mr. Yoder. "My brother loved that woman. He did not deserve what happened to him." Jake paused. "The last time I saw him in his workshop, he showed me what he was working on. He was so proud."

"The cradle," the older man said. "Yes. It was a fine piece, but it was a commission. He had great hopes for making another just like it and filling that cradle."

Jake glanced over at the buggy and then returned his attention to Mr. Yoder. Though he seemed to want to say more, it appeared all he could manage was a nod.

The arrival of a wrecker with CHESTER'S AUTOS emblazoned on the side relieved Jake of the need to respond further.

Henri stepped down from the wrecker and waved to Mary. "Chester missed me," she said. "And he's loaned me the money to fix my car."

"I'm glad," Mary called.

"Got a bad battery?" Henri asked as she walked over to Martha's car.

"I think so." Martha shrugged. "It was fine, and now it won't start."

Mr. Yoder walked over to the wrecker, and Jake followed. Mary watched as the two men offered their opinions to Henri on the fix for Martha's car. The fact that Mr. Yoder drove a buggy apparently did not affect his ability to diagnose issues with a car.

"Mr. Yoder," his wife called from the buggy, "the day is moving on without us."

The older man gave no indication that he'd heard. A moment later, however, he stepped away from the car and joined Mrs. Yoder and their guests in the buggy.

As they set off down the road, Mrs. Yoder's clipped German accent followed them, drowned out finally by the *clip-clop* of the horse's hooves on the paved road. The buggy disappeared over the hill, and a moment later a patrol car appeared.

"That's John," Martha said. "I wonder what he's doing here."

John parked his cruiser and greeted everyone. He walked over to where Henri was putting the finishing touches on the battery replacement. "Need any help?"

Henri gave him a look then peered around the open hood to look at Martha. "Try to start it." When the engine roared to life, she slammed the hood down and looked over at John. "Thank you, but no."

He grinned and walked over to Mary and Jake. "Any news on the investigation?" Mary asked.

"Nothing on the Feds, but the task force is working on this, and there haven't been any more fires, so that's good."

"But?" Jake supplied.

"But all of a sudden we're having trouble getting potential witnesses to cooperate in the Miller explosion investigation."

"Perhaps I could help," Mary said. "They might open up to me. I could ask questions if you'd like."

"There is an official investigation with a task force and the Feds breathing down our necks, which is all the more reason to stay out of it now, Mary," he said gently. "Although a word from you to the Amish about cooperating with us might be helpful."

She tried not to let his statement sting. Did John think she would be anything other than circumspect in her questions? And she would certainly not allow any preconceived notions about what did or did not happen to color her investigation.

"You were all for my sisters and me looking into the fires before. What's changed?"

He sighed. "I'm getting a lot of pressure to get this solved, even though the fires seem to have stopped. And while I appreciate your efforts, I have to limit what I say to you and how much I allow you to be in the loop on the investigations. It's not like it's just my department now."

"Okay, but we've found out some helpful things for you, John. And what about the records Henri turned over to the task force? Isn't that going to help in determining who was near the fires on the nights in question?"

"It will, and if it makes any difference, I put a good word in with her boss to get her back working again." He paused. "Please just leave this to the professionals."

Ouch. And yet this was John's investigation, not hers. He was the police officer, and she was merely a shop owner with a penchant for unravelling mysteries and occasionally solving a crime. She could still ask questions. Unofficially, of course.

"Mary?"

"Yes, of course," she said. "I'll leave the professional questions to the professionals." What she didn't tell him was that if the opportunity allowed for continuing to investigate the fire that led to Caleb being in a coma, she wouldn't hesitate to seize it.

Then a thought occurred. She smiled.

"John," she said sweetly, "I understand that you want us to leave this to the professionals, but haven't you already involved us? As I recall, you've needed our help before. Why wouldn't you need it now?"

He looked surprised. Then his eyes crinkled at the corners. "All right, Mary," he said with a chuckle. "I do see your point. However, please don't get in the middle of an active investigation. The person setting these fires is dangerous. We don't know if the Miller fire is connected to the others or not, but if it is, then the perpetrator is getting more brazen. Be careful. And if you haven't already guessed, I'm telling you this because it comes as a direct order from my boss, okay?"

"Okay, but I'm not Amish, so I'm not a target," she said. "Or am I wrong?"

John let out a long breath. "We thought the first fire was an isolated incident. The second one looked like an argument between competitors, until the facts were more closely examined. Now the man who might have ended up on a short list of potential suspects is lying in a coma from a fire that may also be the work of our arsonist." He paused. "So we don't know have an answer to that question. Any business is at risk right now. If you inadvertently cross this guy, Secondhand Blessings could be next."

Exactly what Eunice Rohrer had told Martha.

Not at all what Mary wanted to hear again. "I see." She gathered her thoughts and continued. "What can we do to protect ourselves?"

"If I knew, I would tell you," he said. "Just be vigilant, be careful, and above all, be mindful of what you say and do, especially around your Amish friends. One of them could be the arsonist."

John checked his watch. "About time for me to be off duty." He reached into his car to throw his hat on the seat then straightened and shrugged. "We'll catch this person, whoever it is. Don't worry about that."

"Don't worry? This has hit way too close to home."

"It could be closer, Mary," he said as he climbed into the driver's seat. "Give thanks it hasn't been." He started the car. "By the way, is Elizabeth with you?"

So that was why he was here. She stepped back so John could close his door then waited until he rolled the window down. "She's at the hospital sitting with Caleb so Jake can be here."

"Ah," he said. "That's exactly something she would do." He rolled up the window, shifted the car into gear, and headed out of the parking lot. Mary watched until the taillights of the cruiser disappeared over the hill.

She returned to the car to find Martha waiting for her and no Jake. "I thought you were leaving, and I was getting a ride home with Jake," she said.

"He was itching to get back to the hospital," Martha said.

"That's a very good idea," Mary said. "Because I think Elizabeth's ride home from the hospital is on his way."

After calling John—Mary was right, he was headed to the hospital—to make sure he could bring Elizabeth home, Martha drove down the road while she listened to Mary relay her conversation with John regarding the task force. "He warned me that the next fire could hit much closer to home. He thinks if we don't stop asking questions, Secondhand Blessings could be next."

"So if we start digging, we might be in danger," Martha said as she signaled to turn into their driveway.

"John was adamant that we leave the investigating to the professionals," Mary said. "There's a task force made up of law enforcement from several cities working on the case."

"And we're just three sisters from Bird-in-Hand who happen to have solved a few mysteries." Martha pulled to a stop in front of the house and turned off the engine. "We've been investigating for a week. I think we can keep our eyes and ears open without getting into too much trouble, don't you?"

Mary climbed out of the car and snatched up her purse. "I think you're right, dear sister," she said with a grin.

"Okay," Martha said. "When Elizabeth gets back let's discuss it."

"That sounds good," Mary said. "I've had two phone calls, and I need to check my messages."

Mary went toward the house, and Martha went down to the shop to retrieve some things from the office. Pal followed her, obviously lonely for some attention. She petted him, told him to sit, and said, "Wait here, boy, and I'll be right back." She unlocked the door and then, with Mary's words of warning in mind, locked it behind her.

After hitting the switch to turn on the lights, she looked around. It never ceased to amaze her that she and her sisters had managed to bring this dream of reviving Secondhand Blessings to fruition.

"We owe it all to You, Lord," she whispered.

Her footsteps echoed in the quiet space, chasing her to the room that served as their workroom. She retrieved the laptop she'd left last night and tucked it under her arm. Out of the corner of her eye, she spied the photograph of her grandbabies that she had printed and framed. That needed to go up to the house too.

Instead of picking it up, however, she sat down in a chair beside the framed photograph and studied it closely. The little ones were growing so fast.

Though it had been more than three years since her husband died unexpectedly of a heart attack, fresh grief rushed through her. "Oh, Chuck, I wish we were sharing this stage of our lives."

Pals' frantic barking and a voice yelling jolted her attention away from her thoughts. Martha gathered up the laptop and photograph and went to see who it was. To her surprise, Abigail Byler was outside the door, with Pal, fur bristling, barking for all he was worth.

CHAPTER TWENTY-TWO

"Call this monster off!" Abigail screamed. "He won't let me near the door."

Martha grabbed Pal's collar, and he quit barking and sat immediately. Abigail, red-faced and sweating, came forward a few feet. "I saw the lights on and thought you were open," she said. She clenched her fists and put them behind her back. "I—I had hoped to...um...speak with Elizabeth. She was so kind to go sit with Caleb, and I thought I would thank her myself."

"Secondhand Blessings is closed right now," Martha told her. "But Elizabeth will be home very soon. We can go to the house and wait for her."

"Thank you," Abigail said. "Perhaps—" Suddenly she shook her head and began walking toward a buggy that was parked on the side of the road a few yards down from the driveway. Why so far away? "I should not have come here. Anna will be angry with me."

"Wait," Martha called after her. "Don't go yet. I would like very much if you would deliver a message to your sister."

Abigail turned around and stopped but said nothing. Martha took a deep breath and let it out slowly.

"I lost my husband. I loved him dearly and even now, with several years passing since then, I sometimes find it hard to believe he's gone." She paused to collect her thoughts then continued. "My sisters have been my lifeline and the best cure I could have found for the pain. So maybe this is for both of you. But please tell Anna that if the worst happens, I promise the Lord will bring her through this. He is faithful to do that. She just needs to find out what comes next for her. That is the key to getting past the heartbreak."

Abigail stood very still. For a moment, Martha didn't think she would respond. Then she said, "My sister is very angry with her husband for accepting his brother into our home. We—my family, my community—are not like the community here in Bird-in-Hand. We respect our *Ordnung*, and we work faithfully to keep its rules and keep ourselves apart from those who have rejected us."

"But Jake never joined the church," protested Martha. "That's why he's not shunned in the community here."

"The fact remains," Abigail said, "that he rejected the church of his forefathers. He can never be accepted in my sister's house."

"Let's go up to the house and wait to speak with Elizabeth," Martha said. "She's who you came to see, and she can help us decide how to proceed."

"There is no proceeding," Abigail said. "Anna is my sister. I will not undermine her." A car passed by on the road, and Abigail looked over at it before returning her attention to Martha. "I must get back. Anna will wonder where I have gone."

Martha held up her hand. "Wait. Surely we can work this out."

Abigail shook her head. "I will not come again. And there is no reason for the police or the fire people to come by anymore. We will not talk to them. We have forgiven the person who did this, and we will now put it behind us."

Martha had no good response, so she merely stared. Finally, words came. "I don't know how to answer this, Abigail, except to say that the police and fire investigators will do their jobs. They won't let this go until they've caught the person or persons responsible for the fires. You should be cooperating with them."

"No."

"Where were you from the time you got back to the farm until the workshop exploded?"

Abigail shrugged. "I live in the dawdy haus on the back of the property. I had no reason to be anywhere else."

"Do you know anything about the reason behind an argument between Caleb and a woman named Julie Bettencourt?"

"I had never heard of her. Until the explosion I heard nothing."

Abigail walked the remaining yards toward the buggy and climbed in. Martha followed her.

"My sister Elizabeth has a friend on that case. His name is John. Let me arrange a meeting with him. No one will have to know that you spoke with him."

Abigail opened her mouth to speak and then closed it again. With a shake of her head, she set the buggy in motion. Martha stood and watched as the buggy disappeared into the distance, then she made the trek back to the house.

With each step, she wondered what she could have said to convince Abigail to talk to John.

Martha had no answers, but she would certainly bring up the questions in the family meeting. She glanced down at her watch and then picked up the pace.

It was time.

Elizabeth stared down at the text on her phone. CHANGE OF PLANS, I'M PICKING YOU UP. AM IN THE WAITING ROOM, NO HURRY, I HAVE A BOOK. AM THINKING OF ICE CREAM.

Elizabeth's heart gave a little flutter before she could remind herself that she wasn't sure she wanted what John might offer her someday. She gathered her purse, said good-bye to Jake, who had arrived just minutes before, and made her way to the ICU waiting room. Sure enough, there was John, just settling into a chair and cracking open a book. She knew he kept one or two in the cruiser for just such occasions as this. Police officers had times when they had to hurry up and wait, just like everybody else.

John's face lit up when he saw her, and he stood. "Elizabeth, you didn't have to come so quickly. I didn't want you to feel like you had to hurry off."

For the first time in months, she felt awkward with him. "I...um...was ready to come, really," she said. "Martha and Mary went home without me?"

He looked a little hurt. "I hope it's okay I told them I could come get you. I didn't think it would matter to you. Does it?"

She hastened to undo her gaffe. "No, no, it's okay." She turned to the exit. "Well, we should get going."

John caught up with her at the elevator and pushed the DOWN button. She kept her eyes on the numbers above the door as they counted up to their floor. When the doors opened, they entered and rode down in silence.

When they exited the building, John put his hand on the small of her back and guided her to a bench away from the sidewalk. When they stopped in front of it, he took her upper arms and gently pushed her until the back of her knees touched the bench and she sat. He sat beside her then and turned to face her.

"All right, Elizabeth," he said. "I'm listening."

Elizabeth kept her head down. This was certainly not helping. Not one bit. Here she was, trying to keep from wanting to be with John, and he had to go and be all sensitive to her feelings. What could she say? *John, I'm upset because if we ever start a relationship and you ask me to marry you I'll have to say no.* She almost laughed out loud at the thought.

"I'm sorry, John," she said. "I've just had a lot on my mind lately, what with the fires and Caleb's coma and Martha trying to decide if she wants to buy a bakery. I think it's all just been a bit too much to take in all at once." There. All of that was the truth, and none of it was as embarrassing as the rest of the truth would be.

"I can understand that," he said. "Which is why I talked to Mary about you three taking some time off the sleuthing and letting us handle it." He nudged her with his elbow. "And when I say 'some' time, I mean all of it."

"I hear you," she said. "I think that's a good idea."

"And?" he prompted.

Uh-oh. "And what?" Elizabeth asked, trying to keep her voice light.

"What's the real problem, Elizabeth? I know it's not just that you're overwhelmed with a mystery. I've seen you involved in cases like this too many times to believe that." He put his finger under her chin and forced her to look at him. "Please tell me what's wrong."

Elizabeth felt her resolve weaken. Then two tears left her eyes. "I just don't know...I just wonder..." she began. She swallowed hard. "John, do you think...I mean, if you ever married someone again..." She felt her face flush. "Would it be hard for you to give up the house or the things you had with Carol?"

She saw from John's face that she'd surprised him with that question. His brows furrowed. "I guess I haven't given it a lot of thought, but I'm pretty sure that if I come to love someone enough to marry her, then she would mean more to me than a house or what's in it." He took her hand. "Besides, the important part of Carol, who she was, what we had together, and my memories of her, are in my heart, not in a house or possessions."

John studied her for a moment. "Let me ask you the same question another way," he said. "What if, heaven forbid, our arsonist torched Secondhand Blessings and your home? Could you and your sisters carry on? Could you rebuild? Could you carry your memories of your parents and grandparents in your hearts, or would they have gone up in smoke?"

"We would rebuild," she said instantly. "No fire on earth could keep us from honoring and remembering our heritage."

"Well then," he said. "I think you've answered your own question."

Elizabeth smiled through her tears. "I think you're right," she said. "Thank you, John, for understanding."

"No problem," he said, standing and pulling her to her feet. "Now can we go get some ice cream? And I want to hear all about this bakery thing and Martha."

Elizabeth couldn't help but laugh. "That is the best idea I've heard in a very long time," she said, taking his arm. She didn't know what the future held with this man, but what was a little ice cream between friends? After all, nobody ever fell in love over ice cream, right?

Mary dusted shelves in the housewares section of Secondhand Blessings on Thursday morning and thought of what transpired at the very late-night meeting of the sisters the night before. Martha's story of Abigail's visit to the store intrigued her the most.

Mary shook her head as she watched the feather duster dance over a wooden salad bowl. It just didn't add up.

"Mama would say you're woolgathering."

She looked up from her work to find Elizabeth watching her. "Mama would be right. I'm thinking about Abigail's visit yesterday, and I just can't make sense of it."

"I don't know what I think yet," Elizabeth said.

Mary considered the irrational feelings she'd had in the early days and weeks after her husband of more than two decades left their marriage for his secretary. Feelings she never acted upon but had nonetheless.

"I want to believe a woman would not try to harm her husband."

Elizabeth shook her head. "We don't know yet whether Anna did that or not."

"No, I know." She set the feather duster down beside the bowl and leaned against the shelf. "And that's what troubles me. I was there just hours before the explosion. Anna was distraught. It was as if she went from being a grown woman to an angry toddler throwing a tantrum at the snap of a finger."

"That's certainly not normal behavior for an adult," Elizabeth conceded. "You said Caleb told you his wife was high strung."

"He did, but I wonder if he was being kind when he described her." She shrugged. "And yet none of it adds up to a woman who would set fires, does it?"

The door opened, and a trio of chattering women stepped inside, preventing further conversation on the subject. Elizabeth gave her a look that said, "We'll discuss this later," and then went off to attend to the shoppers.

But Mary couldn't let the subject go so easily. She'd been there. Had been inside the workshop that had gone up in flames only hours later. Had looked into the eyes of a woman furious over what? A surprise visit from her brother-in-law and his friend?

Or was there more to her anger and histrionics than just a woman who found fault with everything and everyone around her?

Mary grabbed the feather duster and hurried to deposit it in the workroom. With just the three shoppers in the store and

Rachel leading the quilting circle and Martha arriving any time from her dentist appointment, it was the perfect moment to slip out and do a little investigating of her own.

Other than Anna and Abigail, there was another woman who could give insight into what happened on the day of the fire at the Miller farm: Anna and Caleb's neighbor, Bess Yoder.

Though Mrs. Yoder might not want to speak with an Englischer, she could hardly turn her away if she came bearing gifts. It just wasn't done in the Amish community.

Mary removed her apron and hung it on the peg then snatched up a loaf of Martha's banana nut bread from the display. She marched over to the housewares section and picked up a basket made from pieces of wood that had been molded into shape by hand and returned to fill it with bakery treats. "Put this on my tab," she told Elizabeth once the shoppers had gone. "And if you don't mind, I'm going to run an errand. I don't think it'll take long."

Elizabeth chuckled. "You don't have a tab, but all right. What are you going to do with it?"

Mary plucked a jar of local honey off the counter and smiled. "'Pleasant words are as an honeycomb, sweet to the soul, and health to the bones.'"

"Proverbs 16:24. But what does that have to do with where you're planning to take this basket?"

She grinned. "The recipient just might need some sweetening up."

Mary passed Martha as she walked toward her car. "Where are you going?" her sister asked.

"Delivering this to an elderly lady who needs to talk," she told her. "I'll explain when I get back."

She arrived at the Yoder farm to the upraised eyebrows of Benjamin Yoder, who happened to be clearing a patch of weeds near the gate. He stood and gave her a look that told her she'd best have a good reason to be there.

Mary lowered the window, allowing a gust of August heat to invade her vehicle. "I'm here to see Mrs. Yoder. Is she in?"

Mr. Yoder looked past Mary to the basket secured by the seat belt on the seat beside her. "She is, but what business would you be expecting to conduct with her?"

"No business," she told him. "I'm just bringing a basket from the store. I thought perhaps she might need a blessing today."

His harrumph let her know he wasn't buying a bit of it, but he nodded toward the white house at the end of the drive all the same. "You will find her out back likely. She does the wash on Thursdays."

"Thank you."

Before she could roll the window back up, the older man nodded toward the basket. "A word of wisdom if I might?"

"Of course," she said with a smile.

"The next time you seek to pry information from my wife, bring that lavender honey you all carry. It is a particular favorite."

She upped her grin. "I didn't realize your wife liked that kind. I'll keep it in mind." She paused. "If there's a need, that is."

Mr. Yoder's expression never changed. "Oh, Bess does not like it at all, but I do. Keep that in mind. I just might have a thing or two to say as well."

Mary wasn't sure whether he was serious or joking. "Do you have anything to say now? Because I could go get the lavender honey and be back fast."

Still his emotion evaded her, but she could have sworn there was the slightest twinkle in his blue eyes. "Better go talk to Bess. If I think of anything to say, I will let you know."

"Yes, all right."

Mary drove up to the house fully aware that Mr. Yoder was still standing where she left him watching her. She got out of the car, unbuckled the basket, and carried it around the back of the tidy home to find Mrs. Yoder bending over to reach into a laundry basket, her back to Mary.

"Good morning, Mrs. Yoder," she called in an attempt to keep from surprising the old woman.

Her attempt failed miserably. Mrs. Yoder jumped, gave a yelp, and nearly tumbled into the basket. Mary set her gift on the ground and hurried to right the Amish woman.

"You gave me a terrible fright, girl." Mrs. Yoder straightened her kapp then glared in Mary's direction. "Why would you do that to an old woman?"

"I'm so sorry. I didn't want to surprise you so..." She shrugged and hurried back to retrieve the gift. "So anyway, I just wanted to bring you a little something from the store."

Mrs. Yoder looked at the basket with a skeptical eye then frowned at Mary. "Why would you do that?"

Okay, so not the reception she'd hoped for, but definitely the one she should have expected. Mary took a long breath and let it out slowly.

"You've been so kind to the Millers. First to both of them by providing meals, and then to Anna during her husband's illness. I just thought I would bring you a token of—"

"It is what we do." She stepped around Mary to reach for a piece of clothing from the pile. "We do not expect reward for doing what is our duty." After a glance at the basket and then back up at Mary, she shook her head. "Nor do we accept it…at least, not usually."

Mary suppressed a smile. She said, "Jakob Miller and I were the last ones other than his wife to see Caleb before the explosion. I wonder if you could spare just a minute to help me understand."

"Understand what?" Mrs. Yoder asked as she reached down to pick up a pair of dark trousers and add them to the clothesline.

"Understand what happened," Mary said gently. "Caleb was so proud when he showed us the cradle he was building and said he would be making one for the children he and Anna would have. And he had just promised to make an easel for me like the one in the workshop."

At the mention of the cradle and easel, Mrs. Yoder's brows rose. Still, she continued her rhythm of reaching for laundry, hanging it, and then doing it all over again. Mary set her basket down and began to help. Though Mrs. Yoder said nothing, Mary took it as an encouraging sign that she didn't tell her to stop.

Finally, when the laundry basket was empty, Mrs. Yoder snatched it up and walked back to the house. Not knowing whether to follow nor not, Mary picked up her basket and chose to shadow her all the way to the back door.

When they reached the house Mrs. Yoder looked down at the basket Mary was carrying, seemingly surveying its contents, and then back up at Mary.

Mrs. Yoder gave her one more appraising look. Then came a curt nod as she opened the back door. "You will come in for a minute only."

CHAPTER TWENTY-THREE

A minute was all Mary needed, though she would take longer if she could manage it. She followed Mrs. Yoder inside and gave thanks that she had been allowed in.

The neat-as-a-pin home smelled of sunshine and lemons, and every surface gleamed. Mary set the basket on the table, and Mrs. Yoder snatched it up.

"Your sister's banana nut bread is very good." She looked up at Mary. "Would she share her recipe?"

"I, um, well, I'm sure she wouldn't mind," Mary said, not sure at all but hoping she was right.

Mrs. Yoder made short work of cutting two thick slices of the bread and plating them. She took the plates and the honey to the table and nodded to Mary. "Sit there."

She did as she was told while Mrs. Yoder bustled about making coffee in what Mary's children would call a very modern-looking French press. By the time her hostess arrived at the table with two steaming cups, the entire kitchen smelled gloriously like richly roasted coffee.

Mrs. Yoder took a seat across from her and stared until Mary was convinced she would not speak. Rather than attempt to fill the silence with conversation, Mary merely smiled and reached for her cup.

"Oh," she exclaimed after taking a sip of the luscious brew. "This coffee is delicious."

"Danki." Mrs. Yoder reached for the honey and applied it liberally to her coffee. Then she took a sip and set her cup back down. She appeared pleased with the coffee and, from Mary's perspective, in no hurry to speak any further.

Then, slowly, she began.

"'For the word of God is quick, and powerful, and sharper than any twoedged sword, piercing even to the dividing asunder of soul and spirit, and of the joints and marrow, and is a discerner of the thoughts and intents of the heart.'"

Was this a Bible quiz? "Hebrews 4:12," Mary told her as she took a sip of coffee.

Mrs. Yoder lifted one shoulder as if to say she wasn't surprised that Mary knew the verse. "You have asked for an answer, but perhaps you will not find it with me. There is only One who knows everything."

"'For nothing is secret, that shall not be made manifest; neither any thing hid, that shall not be known and come abroad.'"

To Mary's surprise, Mrs. Yoder showed the beginnings of a smile. "Luke 8:17."

"Someone knows something, Mrs. Yoder. We could sit here all morning exchanging Bible verses, but that doesn't help answer the question of what happened to Caleb Miller." She paused, only slightly regretting her impertinence. "I've known him since he was a boy."

Unexpected tears swam in her eyes. Mary picked up her fork to take a bite of banana nut bread in an attempt to hide her emotions.

"When he was born, I was there," Mrs. Yoder said. "Caleb, he was a healthy boy and the image of his father. Some say he stole that health from his mother, for she never truly recovered."

Mrs. Yoder's expression was far away now, her eyes focused somewhere other than in the kitchen. Then, in a heartbeat, she returned.

After a bite of bread, she nodded. "Yes, I must have this recipe."

Mary kept her silence. There was no need to answer. Plus, she sensed that Mrs. Yoder just might be sizing her up to see what she would do with the quiet.

Though she itched to speak, to beg Mrs. Yoder to tell what she knew, Mary merely took polite bites of banana nut bread and washed them down with the occasional sip of coffee. When she was done, she paused only a moment.

"Thank you for your hospitality, but my sisters will be wondering what is taking so long."

She rose and picked up her empty plate and cup and took them to the sink to wash. Through it all, Mrs. Yoder said nothing.

"Mrs. Classen, she raised good girls," she finally said as Mary was drying her hands on the towel. "I know you mean well, Mary, but you will not find the answers you are seeking by asking an old woman like me."

Mary carefully folded the towel just as she found it and returned it to its place on the drainboard. "Before me, you were the last to see Anna on the day of the explosion. I only hoped that maybe something she said in that visit could help."

"Help to prove her guilty of arson or murder?" Mrs. Yoder shook her head. "No. Of being a woman who fancies herself always right and just, yes." She paused. "But you already knew this."

"I did."

"It was wise of her father to send Abigail to help her." She picked at the remains of the banana nut bread on her plate but did not take another bite.

"Tell me about Abigail."

A smile rose. "Had I a daughter I would wish her to be like that one. Kind, so full of joy, and such a comfort to her younger sister."

Mary made one last attempt to get information on what might have happened before they returned to the farm. "And neither of them said or did anything during their last visit with you that would provide any hint of what was to come later that day?"

Mrs. Yoder furrowed her silver brows. "Of course not. I would have sent some sort of warning to Caleb. But there was nothing." She paused and then slowly shook her head. "I have been over this more times than I can tell you, and I can find no reason for it."

Mary nodded. "As have I," she said. "But we need to know why that workshop exploded just a few hours after we left. And why two other businesses were also targeted."

"*Gott* has His reasons, and that is enough for me."

"Yes, that is true," Mary said, "but I spent time in that workshop and saw nothing that would make me believe it was in danger of an explosion. No fumes, nothing." She paused to take a deep breath and then let it out slowly. "And Jakob Miller is my friend. He has been since we were children. His brother is badly hurt, and he has questions. I want to provide him with answers."

Mrs. Yoder was silent.

Mary forged on. "By now you've heard that the police believe the fire at the Miller farm could be related to fires at other Amish-owned businesses."

From the expression on the older woman's face, Mary thought perhaps she had not. Or if she did know, she was doing a good job of hiding it.

"Anyone in the community could be next, Mrs. Yoder." She paused to let that sink in then put on a smile. "Thank you again for your hospitality. I will speak to Martha about sharing the recipe for the banana nut bread."

Mary left Mrs. Yoder sitting at the table and returned to her car to find Jake waiting for her. Mr. Yoder was nowhere to be seen.

"Is everything all right?" she asked him.

Jake crossed his arms over his chest and shook his head. "I was about to ask you the same thing. I saw your car parked here and wondered what was going on."

She smiled. "I was doing a little detective work."

"And?"

"And thanks to Martha's banana nut bread I was able to convince Mrs. Yoder to talk to me. I'm not sure she's told me everything, but I believe her when she says that nothing in her conversation with Anna and Abigail foretold what would happen just a few hours later."

He let out a long breath. "I'm surprised she told you anything at all."

"Me too." She paused. "Did you know she was there when Caleb was born?"

Jake frowned. "No, but I was just a kid. I didn't care about the grown-ups who came to the house. I was too excited about my brother being born." His expression softened. "He was all cheeks with hardly any hair, and I wondered when he was going to look like a real boy."

His voice cracked, and he looked way. "I'm sorry. I'm a doctor. I deal with these kinds of things all the time."

Mary reached over to touch his sleeve. "But not when they happen to your brother."

Jake managed a nod but said nothing. Mary decided to give him a moment to compose himself by continuing the update of her visit.

"I told her that anyone could be next. She didn't say anything, but I could tell by her expression that that concerned her."

"It should concern anyone who fits the profile, but they are so stubborn." He paused. "I'm sorry. I just get so frustrated. If they would talk to law enforcement instead of turning their backs—sometimes literally. ..."

Silence fell between them. "I'm sorry, Jake, but I need to get back to the store," she finally said.

"Yes, of course. Thank you for helping me try to get some answers, Mary."

"I'm looking for answers too."

He reached out to touch her sleeve. "And for listening."

Mary's phone rang, and she reached for it. "Elizabeth? Something wrong?"

"The store is on fire, Mary. It's on fire!"

CHAPTER TWENTY-FOUR

M ary raced to the store, following the plume of black smoke that rose on the horizon. By the time she reached the rise on the hill and saw the building up ahead, the smoke was gone, but the fire truck and police cars were not.

She pulled past the fire truck and stopped her car in front of the house then ran to the shop. Firefighters were winding up their hoses as John and another police officer chatted with Elizabeth and Martha. Mary ran to her sisters. "What happened?"

"I was in the office, and Martha was in the store," Elizabeth said. "Something flashed out of the corner of my eye, and I stood up to get a better look. That's when I saw the fire."

"Started in a trash can hauled up close to the building," John said.

Jake came running up to join them as Elizabeth nodded to the area where the firefighters were still standing. "I heard a scream, so I have to assume the arsonist was wounded when she set the fire."

"She?" Mary asked excitedly. "You know it's a she?"

"Our perpetrator should be easy to spot," John told her. "Thanks to Elizabeth's quick thinking."

"I called 911 and ran out to grab the hose. When I made the turn around the side of the house, I saw an Amish woman running away."

"Anna," Jake said. "It had to be."

"I thought so too, but Anna is a small woman. The one running away was bigger than she is."

"The woman got away?" Mary asked.

"Nope," John said. "You might want to give Pal an extra treat tonight, Mary."

"Pal? I don't understand," Mary said.

Martha spoke up. "Do you remember when I told you that last night Pal wouldn't let Abigail near the door of the shop?" At Mary's nod, she continued. "When the woman ran away, Pal was right behind her."

John pointed to the two-way radio on his shoulder. "I just heard he's got her holed up in Silas Fischer's barn, in the hayloft. I expect we'll get a look at her pretty soon."

"And the fire?" Mary asked. "Was anything harmed?"

"Thank the Lord, no," Martha said. "Instead of igniting the building, the flames ended up setting the dead tree outside the workroom on fire."

"So that's what all the smoke was." Mary breathed a sigh of relief. "I was terrified that we would lose everything we've worked so hard for."

A moment later, a squad car pulled up in front of them and stopped. The officer rolled down the window. "I have her in the back. She's feisty. Tried to punch me."

He rolled down the back window to show an angry Abigail Byler restrained by handcuffs. "Abigail?" Mary moved closer. "You? Why?"

Abigail scowled at her. "You are so stupid, Mary Baxter. I was meant to be with Caleb. He knew it, and so did Anna.

But our father thought Anna needed a husband as soon as possible, so he convinced Caleb to marry her. To marry the wrong Byler."

"You were hoping we'd blame her," Jake said. "You wanted her to go to jail."

When Abigail said nothing, Elizabeth stepped in. "What was the purpose of all those clothes in the dawdy haus? Were those Anna's?"

She shrugged. "I replaced the clothes in her suitcase with Englisch clothes then alerted the police that she would be at the bus station and running away. The idiot found the clothes and packed her own again." She smirked. "But they still caught her at the bus station, didn't they?"

Mary shook her head. "But why, Abigail? How could you dislike your own sister so much?"

Abigail's face grew dark with anger. "Just because your sisters are so perfect, Mary Classen. Are you telling me you've never been shortchanged because of them? My sister, the beautiful baby of the family, always got everything, and I got nothing. She got the best, and I got the worst. Her getting Caleb was the last straw."

"Get her out of here," John told the officer. "Make sure she gives a statement."

"I have got a statement for you," Abigail said. "Caleb Miller was supposed to be mine. Jake, you know Anna wasn't the one for him. Tell them that."

Jake shook his head. "Not only will I not tell them that, I'm going to do everything I can to find some way to have a relationship with my brother's wife." His mouth trembled as he said, "Whether Caleb lives or dies, I'm going to build some bridges in this community."

Caleb regained consciousness on Saturday and was moved out of ICU on Monday. Jake and Anna were negotiating a fragile truce that Mary hoped would grow stronger from their mutual love of Caleb. The store was closed over the weekend but opened up on Monday morning as usual. Mary was busy sweeping up in the workroom when she heard a tap at the door. She looked up to see Julie Bettencourt waiting there. "Come in," she told her. "I didn't expect to see you here."

"I hope you don't mind," Julie said. "Martha told me you were back here. I wanted to apologize. I caused a lot of trouble and ran, and I wanted to tell you why."

"I think I know." Mary nodded toward the workroom. "I need to apologize too. I took something of yours when Bill and I were there looking at wood, and I need to return it." She retrieved the photo and handed it to her.

Julie smiled. "Tom's cradle." Her eyes misted. "I had hoped to give it to Tom and his wife before their baby was born. It's a replica of one Tom had hoped to build someday. His father designed it. Anyway, the original cradle was ruined years ago, and now the one Caleb was building is gone too."

"So the big project you were doing with Caleb was a cradle for your supervisor?"

"Yes," she said. "He's a dear man. I couldn't have done any of what I've done in rebuilding the company without him."

Mary smiled. "That's really thoughtful of you," she said. "And I bet that Caleb will be able to build another one for you in a few months."

"I hope so," Julie said. "And I won't even ask how you got the photograph."

Mary grinned. "Probably better that you don't."

The next day, Mary drove up the drive to the Miller farm, not knowing what to expect. Jake's text had been brief. Just a quick request to come and see him before he left. So she agreed, and now here she was in front of the home where less than two weeks ago a tragedy had occurred.

The black smudge where the workshop had been was now cleared off and the slab washed clean. A pile of lumber was stacked in the barn, alerting her to the possibility that the workshop might be rebuilt. Mary knew it would be a community project and would be done quickly and with a lot of camaraderie and delicious food.

Jake stepped out of the house and walked toward her with a smile. "Thank you for coming," he said. "I didn't want to leave without saying goodbye, but I wanted to show you something first. Will you come with me?"

She climbed out of her car and followed him to the dawdy haus. The old furniture was gone, and the place was now empty.

"What's going on here?"

He shrugged. "I'm making room," he said. "I'm coming back here, Mary. I don't belong in New York City. Bird-in-Hand is my home."

"But what about your medical practice?"

"I can practice here. It'll take a little while to get my credentials here, but when I do, I'm set." He walked with her to the back window that overlooked the pasture. Someone was plowing. Possibly Mr. Yoder or Mr. Rohrer, though it was impossible to tell from this distance.

"It's never too late to start over, Jake," she told him. "How do Caleb and Anna feel about you being here?"

"They're willing to give it a try," he said. "Caleb tried very hard to persuade me to give up medicine and join him in the family business, but I know what I was made for, what my passion is." He smiled at her. "A person has to be true to himself, right?"

She gave him a hug. "Right."

"There's just something about home that's better than anywhere else, isn't there?" Jake said, returning her hug. "Dreams take you away, but they always bring you back home, don't they?"

"They do," Mary said. "Stop by the store and see me when you get back."

"I promise," he said as he walked her to her car then waved as she drove away.

Mary got a mile down the road with Jake's words chasing her. She thought about the gallery in Philly and the difficult decision she'd been trying to make, and she suddenly realized it really wasn't all that difficult. She pulled over and made a call.

"Augie," she said when the art dealer's voice mail picked up. "I appreciate your generous offer, but I'm going to have to pass. I may do an occasional barn and buggy picture, but that's not what I want to be known for. I'm going to be true to my heart and my art. If I never get in a gallery, so be it. Of course, you can always check out my booth at the art fair next time you're in town."

She hung up with a grin and pulled back on the road toward home. A few minutes later, she stepped inside her house to find her sisters seated at the kitchen table. As she walked in, they both stopped talking.

"What?" she asked.

"We've been waiting for you," Elizabeth said. "Martha has some news."

"And so do I," Mary said. "But you first, Martha."

"I am not buying the bakery," she said. "It's just not the right time. I would miss you two terribly, and I just don't want to give up what I've already got here."

Mary grinned. "That's wonderful news."

"I thought so too," Elizabeth said. "Now what's yours?"

"I'm not going to paint buggies and barns for big bucks."

Martha and Elizabeth exchanged a confused look. "I have no idea what you're talking about," Martha said. "But congratulations?" She and Elizabeth burst out laughing.

Mary joined in then she sobered. "I suppose I did forget to let you know about that. But I have even better news. Jake is coming back to live in Bird-in-Hand. Moving his medical practice too." She paused. "He says a dream will lead you home."

Her sisters smiled. "I think he's right," Martha said.

"I know he is," Elizabeth agreed.

A NOTE FROM THE AUTHOR

I love art fairs. On top of that, I raised an artist. So starting this book with our resident artist, Mary Baxter, plying her wares at the monthly art fair in Lancaster was so much fun. Even more fun was considering that Mary could be painting barns and buggies for big bucks, as she puts it. As Mary learns, however, there is much more to the talents God gives you than turning them into a way to pay the rent. I loved exploring that idea and giving Mary options. The same could be said for Martha and her bakery. At the end of the day, the choices that were made were to keep doing what God told them to do rather than chasing a dream that wasn't properly timed. That really resonated with me, and I hope it resonates with you.

Kathleen Y'Barbo

ABOUT THE AUTHOR

Kathleen Y'Barbo is a multiple Carol Award and RITA nominee and bestselling author of more than one hundred books with over two million copies of her books in print in the US and abroad. A tenth-generation Texan and certified paralegal, she is a member of the Texas Bar Association Paralegal Division, Texas A&M Association of Former Students and the Texas A&M Women Former Students (Aggie Women), Texas Historical Society, Novelists Inc., and American Christian Fiction Writers. She would also be a member of the Daughters of the American Republic, Daughters of the Republic of Texas, and a few others if she would just remember to fill out the paperwork that Great Aunt Mary Beth has sent her more than once.

When she's not spinning modern-day tales about her wacky Southern relatives, Kathleen inserts an ancestor or two into her historical and mystery novels as well. Recent book releases include bestselling *The Pirate Bride,* set in 1700s New Orleans and Galveston, and its sequel, *The Alamo Bride,* set in 1836 Texas, which feature a few well-placed folks from history and a family tale of adventure on the high seas and on the coast of Texas. She also writes (mostly) relative-free cozy mystery novels for Guideposts Books.

Kathleen and her hero-in-combat-boots husband have their own surprise love story that unfolded on social media a few years back. They make their home just north of Houston, Texas, and are the parents and in-laws of a blended family of Texans, Okies, and one very adorable Londoner.

To find out more about Kathleen or connect with her through social media, check out her website at kathleenybarbo.com.

MORE TO THE STORY

The Lancaster Art Market, which is held the first Friday (Saturday in our story) of the month in Lancaster, showcases the art of many of the area's most talented citizens. From paintings to textiles, and everything in between, the art fair is designed to bring handmade goods to buyers and to introduce art to the community.

If you're looking for a larger venue with more exhibits and art, check out the Fine Arts Festival at Long's Park. Held every Labor Day weekend, the festival attracts over 11,000 visitors each year and has been declared one of America's Top Fifty festivals. All proceeds sold from tickets for this event benefit the area's Summer Music Series.

FRESH FROM MARTHA'S KITCHEN

Martha's Banana Nut Bread

2 cups flour	1 cup sugar
1 teaspoon baking powder	2 eggs
1 teaspoon salt	2 medium bananas, ripe
½ cup shortening	and mashed
1 teaspoon vanilla	½ cup chopped nuts

Sift together flour, baking powder, and salt. In a mixing bowl, blend together shortening and vanilla and sugar, then cream with a mixer until light and fluffy. Add eggs one at a time then add the mashed bananas. Gradually add dry ingredients until mixed. Stir in nuts.

Grease and flour a loaf pan and fold in mixture. Bake at 350 degrees for 1 hour.

Read on for a sneak peek of another exciting book
in the Mysteries of Lancaster County series!

Bird's Eye View
by Shaen Layle and Nancy Mehl

Martha Classen Watts took in a deep breath of crisp September air. Although she'd been reluctant to join her sister Elizabeth in purchasing a "just because" gift for their younger sister, at the moment she was glad she'd agreed. Mary was so excited and happy.

"So what do you think?" Elizabeth asked. "Did you ever imagine we'd spend our Friday night doing something like this?"

"No," Martha replied, "but Mary's wanted it for so long. ..."

"I have," Mary said with a grin. "I'm really grateful for the gift. And honestly surprised the two of you were willing to get inside a hot-air balloon."

Martha looked around her. They weren't too high yet, but their distance from the ground still made her a little queasy. She was thrilled for Mary, but she would be relieved when they landed.

She looked over at their pilot, Norman Tatlock. He'd informed them that his friends called him Stormin' Norman. Martha wasn't too crazy about the nickname. Right now, she'd rather be riding with *Reliable Norman* or *Trustworthy Norman*. She smiled to herself. Probably not nicknames most men would want.

Norman had gone over the parts of the balloon before they took off. The big balloon itself was called the *envelope*. The basket where they were seated was a *gondola*. Then, of course, there were the burners that fueled the envelope. Martha appreciated his attempt to educate them, but she was more interested in the safety aspects of their journey. She was grateful to see that he'd checked the wind currents before they left, doing several calculations, making certain it was safe to go up.

The Lancaster Balloon Festival was a yearly event held in Bird-in-Hand. There were races, along with lots of other events. Food trucks came in from all around to feed the crowds that showed up. Tonight, there was a bonfire and s'mores. Although the sisters had driven over to watch the festival last year, this was the first time they'd booked a ride. It was extremely expensive, but Officer John Marks, a friend of the sisters, had talked his buddy Norman into giving them a deal. It was still a hit on the pocketbook but worth it. The sisters had been working hard at their store, Secondhand Blessings. They deserved a reward that felt special, and this certainly qualified.

As other balloons began to leave the ground around them, Martha gasped. The sky was dotted with colorful envelopes, each softly glowing and lit from within. The sight took her breath away.

When the ground crew had released the cables that held their balloon to the earth, she'd almost told them not to let go, that she'd changed her mind. But now she was glad she'd stayed. This was incredible.

"It's beautiful, isn't it?" Elizabeth asked. "I had no idea it would be this—"

"Awesome?" Mary finished for her. "Brian promised me we'd do this someday, but it never happened."

Martha put her arm around her sister. "But here you are. You made it, and you didn't need Brian." Brian was Mary's ex-husband. His infidelity had destroyed their marriage and devastated Mary, but in the six years since she had grown stronger and more independent. Martha was proud of her.

Mary nodded. "I did, thanks to both of you."

Norman pulled a cord that opened a valve and sent more propane to the burners, causing the envelope to rise higher. Although it was dusk, Martha could still see the people on the ground gathered to watch the balloons take off. Mary and Elizabeth waved at them, but Martha was busy staring at Norman. She'd noticed quite a bit of drinking at the festival. She worried that he may have imbibed. Why hadn't she asked him about that before they took off?

Elizabeth scooted closer to her on the bench-like seat inside the gondola. "Everything will be all right," she whispered. "John wouldn't have recommended Norman unless he was certain we'd be safe."

"How did you know I was thinking about that?" Martha asked.

"It wasn't hard. You're staring daggers at him."

Martha took a deep breath and let it out slowly. She smiled at Elizabeth. "I didn't mean to. Why am I such a worrywart?"

"It's because you care. You want to keep us all safe."

Martha grunted. "I guess you're right."

"Just sit back and enjoy this, Martha. We might not ever get the chance to do it again."

At Elizabeth's words, Martha settled back in her seat, determined to appreciate this unique experience. She looked around again at the other balloons. Most of the envelopes were made of brightly colored material sewn together in geometric patterns. Then there was one that looked like a big blue dog. Their own balloon was striped with vivid rainbow colors. It was certainly eye-catching.

While Elizabeth and Martha looked down at the countryside below them, Mary chatted with Norman. Finally, she sat down on the bench opposite them.

"Did you know that some balloons can seat thirty people?" she asked.

"Thirty?" Martha repeated. "You'd never get me on something like that."

"Norman says hot air balloons are very safe. There haven't been many serious accidents."

Martha snorted. "It's not like Norman would tell you something different."

Norman pulled the cord again, and they rose even higher. Martha took another deep breath and watched her sisters, who had spotted some deer in a field below them. Elizabeth joined Mary on the other side of the gondola so they could watch them. Martha stayed where she was. Moving around made her nervous.

As they drifted farther east, they passed over Bird-in-Hand. The town looked so different from the air. People below stopped and stared at them. Some even waved. Martha finally gave in and waved back. It seemed a little silly, but after doing it a few times, she had to admit it was fun. As if they were sharing this unique experience with others.

Norman finally told them he was heading back. "I think we'll be able to land at the festival grounds," he said. "There's not enough wind to throw us off course."

Martha felt a twinge of regret to hear that their adventure was nearing its end. Elizabeth was right. This could be the only time they'd ever get to ride in a balloon. As they began to circle back, Martha continued watching the ground below them, though it was getting a little harder to see in the waning light. She could still make out houses, fields, and farm animals. They passed Rachel Fischer's house, but no one was outside. Rachel was Amish and had been a good friend to the sisters over the years, even helping out in the store when they needed assistance.

They crossed the Fischers' fields and before long passed over their own property. Mary and Elizabeth leaned over the side of the gondola so they could see their house as they floated by. Martha focused on the scenery below her, not willing to move from her spot. Lights twinkled from farmhouses nestled inside groves of trees turning autumn colors, a promise of winter on the way. Some of the fields had already been harvested. It seemed as if the land was preparing for rest. It felt so peaceful.

As they drifted toward an abandoned hardware store not far from the highway, Martha noticed a couple of cars in the parking lot with their headlights on, providing enough illumination for Martha to see a man and a woman standing in the lot facing each other. As she watched, it didn't take long to realize that something was wrong. The man grabbed the woman and began to struggle with her. Martha wasn't sure, but she thought she saw the woman look up. Was she searching for help? Then the man raised his hand, brought it down, and the woman fell to the ground. Shocked, Martha's natural reaction was to yell at the man, but she thought better of it when she realized he couldn't possibly hear her.

The man pulled the woman up from the ground and hurriedly pushed her inside one of the vehicles. Before the man got behind the wheel, Martha thought he might have glanced up too. Had he seen them? Martha quickly pulled back.

"Hey," she said loudly, trying to be heard over the sound of the burners. "Something's wrong."

Elizabeth turned around. "Did you say something?" she asked.

Martha pointed over the side of the gondola. "I think a woman is being kidnapped."

She turned back and watched as the man sped off. They were soon out of Martha's sight, the hardware store hidden behind a copse of trees. Although she'd tried hard to spot something that would help her describe the man or his car, it was nearly impossible. She hadn't been able to clearly see the woman's face either. She felt so frustrated. How could she tell the police anything that would help them rescue that poor woman?

Elizabeth and Mary scooted toward Martha and were trying to look over her side of the gondola when Norman reminded them about too much weight on one side.

"I need one of you to move toward the middle," he said, frowning. "You're throwing off the balance."

"We've got to do something," Martha said as her sisters moved away from her.

"It's getting dark," Mary said. "Are you sure you saw someone being abducted? Maybe they were just having an argument."

"Of course I'm sure," Martha snapped. "I think I know the difference between an argument and a kidnapping. I'm not prone to making up stories, you know."

"We know that," Elizabeth said soothingly.

"Call John," Martha said to Elizabeth. "Tell him to get to that hardware store. I'm sure the woman's car is still there."

"Sorry, ladies," Norman said. "No phone calls while we're in the air. Aviation law. You'll have to wait until we land."

"Don't worry," Elizabeth said. "When we get down, we'll call John. You can tell him what you saw, okay?'

"We have to find her," Martha said. "Even though I couldn't see her very well, I think she saw me looking at her. I have to wonder if she's hoping I'll help her."

Elizabeth patted Martha's hand. "We'll check it out. Don't worry."

Mary chimed in her agreement. "John will know what to do."

Martha was quiet as they headed back. She didn't want to ruin the experience for Mary by insisting she'd seen something sinister unfold on the ground below them, but she had no plans to back down. She was certain the woman had been taken against her will. She'd been kidnapped, and Martha might be the only person who could save her.

A NOTE FROM THE EDITORS

We hope you enjoyed this volume of the Mysteries of Lancaster County series, created by the Books and Inspirational Media Division of Guideposts. We are a nonprofit organization that touches millions of lives every day through products and services that inspire, encourage, help you grow in your faith, and celebrate God's love in every aspect of your daily life.

Thank you for making a difference with your purchase of this book, which helps fund our many outreach programs to military personnel, prisons, hospitals, nursing homes, and educational institutions. To learn more, visit GuidepostsFoundation.org.

We also maintain many useful and uplifting online resources. Visit Guideposts.org to read true stories of hope and inspiration, access OurPrayer network, sign up for free newsletters, download free e-books, join our Facebook community, and follow our stimulating blogs.

To learn about other Guideposts publications, including the bestselling devotional *Daily Guideposts*, go to ShopGuideposts .org, call (800) 932-2145, or write to Guideposts, PO Box 5815, Harlan, Iowa 51593.

Find more inspiring fiction in these best-loved Guideposts series!

Secrets of Wayfarers Inn

Fall back in history with three retired schoolteachers who find themselves owners of an old warehouse-turned-inn that is filled with hidden passages, buried secrets and stunning surprises that will set them on a course to puzzling mysteries from the Underground Railroad.

Sugarcreek Amish Mysteries

Be intrigued by the suspense and joyful "aha" moments in these delightful stories. Each book in the series brings together two women of vastly different backgrounds and traditions, who realize there's much more to the "simple life" than meets the eye.

Mysteries of Martha's Vineyard

Come to the shores of this quaint and historic island and dig into a cozy mystery. When a recent widow inherits a lighthouse just off the coast of Massachusetts, she finds exciting adventures, new friends, and renewed hope.

Patchwork Mysteries

Discover that life's little mysteries often have a common thread in a series where every novel contains an intriguing mystery centered around a quilt located in a beautiful New England town.

Mysteries of Silver Peak

Escape to the historic mining town of Silver Peak, Colorado, and discover how one woman's love of antiques helps her solve mysteries buried deep in the town's checkered past.

**To learn more about these books,
visit Guideposts.org/Shop**